LIVING IN THE TRINITY

LIVING IN THE TRINITY

Alastair Redfern

2018

Living in the Trinity - Published by the Rev. Dr. Ashish Amos of the Indian Society for Promoting Christian Knowledge (ISPCK), Post Box 1585, Kashmere Gate, Delhi-110006.

Online order: http://ispck.org.in/book.php

Also available on amazon.in

ISBN: 978-81-8465-656-5

Laser typeset by

ISPCK, Post Box 1585, 1654, Madarsa Road, Kashmere Gate, Delhi-110006 • *Tel:* 23866323

e-mail: ashish@ispck.org.in • ella@ispck.org.in
website: www.ispck.org.in

Contents

Preface

Contemporary western society is often portrayed as 'secular', and displaying a high degree of religious illiteracy. Thus the doctrine of the Trinity can be seen as an anachronistic, incomprehensible notion, three persons as one does not make sense to modern scientific thinking.

Within mainstream Christianity, there is a lively recognition of Jesus as the key to the gospel, and strong strands of a Pentecostal movement bathing in the light of the Spirit. 'The Fatherhood' of God can be contested both on grounds of gender sensitivities, and because the role and authority of parents is diminishing in many sectors of society. These different emphases indicate considerable division and difference within Christian witness and identity. The desire to make immediate connections with contemporary contexts also serves to relegate the doctrine of the Trinity to the area of more obscure traditions.

Given such a landscape, there is an important need for a re-engagement with the doctrine of the Trinity, as the foundation of the Christian Gospel, and the primary formative force of worship and witness. This book invites consideration of this doctrine in the light of contemporary issues in modern society, and tries to highlight the important missionary moment for refocusing upon God as Father, Son and Holy Spirit: three persons, One God.

Introduction

In secular terms, we live in an age of experience. Human thinking, feeling and aspiration are the markers and guides for individual identity and social organisation. This world is expressed through 'Human rights'. Radically inclusive in rhetoric, as per United Nations declarations, but in fact a mask for the widely documented fact that beneath this 'noise' more and more people are falling into poverty and exclusion. The 'wholeness' of human rights discourse masks the ever deepening divisions and fractures within society, and the accompanying rise in levels of 'stress' for individuals trying to navigate these confusing and challenging currents.

The response of much of Christianity in the West has been to affirm this liberal agenda of 'inclusion' while finding a pastoral role in ministering to the stresses and strains being experienced. In theological terms, an emphasis upon 'incarnation' - embodiment which can be observed, experienced and measured. Doctrine and worship then become focussed on this particular arena of human living; issues are around identity and experience, love and hope, that can be tasted and trusted.

Of course these ways of expressing the Christian hope are crucial and foundational. But the Gospel of Jesus Christ is distinctive amongst all such human systems and endeavours by giving prime place to 'The Resurrection of the dead' (Paul in Acts 17), through the Atonement in Christ, which mysteriously and miraculously transforms sin, failure, limitation, darkness and death into new and everlasting life – as sheer gift. This gift transforms human endeavour into the stuff of glory. It is recognised and received in the life of God as Trinity: Father, Son and Holy Spirit.

The chapters which follow try to explore this mystery of divine life as the reality of creation which human beings are made to inhabit. Participation in the life of the Trinity is how human beings can live most fully within the realities of creation – with all its pressures and its potentialities.

The complexities and challenges can be held by 'faith' in a process that is always available for tasting and testing. This openness is too easily not noticed because of a strong tendency to focus on smaller, more defensive strategies and systems – which in fact create shadows and barriers when disconnected from the power and purposes of the life of the Trinity.

The key is worship properly understood and practiced. Joining in the refrain of the angels, Holy Holy, Holy.

1

Living in the Trinity

From 3 to 2 to 1: A Mathematical Challenge

Christianity lives in an important paradox in the contemporary world. At one level a faith in One God who is known as Father, Son and Holy Spirit seems to be nonsensical. If God is one, why such complexity? Many begin to presuppose a religious plot to keep power and control of such faith in the hands of a few who might be able to articulate ingenious justifications for what seems on the surface to be an absurdity – an insult to human intelligence. This seems especially to be the case when so many people are increasingly conscious of challenges in the area of relationships. The Christian mystery of the Trinity can seem to further distance ordinary human experience from orthodox teaching and assumptions.

However, despite this critique in the name of reason, logic and recognisable human experience, this same world faces enormous challenges in terms of diversity, and the deep incompatibilities which seem to exist between different viewpoints and experiences. Reason can suggest all kinds of 'answers' and approaches to diversity, but the tensions seem to become increasingly marked and intransigent. Obvious examples would include the constant struggles of Government, or of the United Nations in politics, or, at a more individual level, recognition of the bewildering varieties of therapies for more personal problems of incoherence and isolation.

A common factor to both of these elements of the paradox – the incomprehensible mystery of a Trinitarian God, and the continuing challenge of diversities – is the predominance of the binary way of thinking that science has strengthened through mathematics, as well as through common deductive analysis. Of course there is a binary foundation to what appears to be reality: heaven and earth: male and female: light and dark: land and sea: creator and creation. In popular language people deal with 'this' and 'that' – a simple way of distinguishing different elements that have to be noticed, handled and developed.

But the key element to the apparently clarificatory thinking of a binary approach to life, is the issue of how different elements relate to each other. In classical theology, St Augustine writes about the Father and the Son, with the Spirit being the love between them. He also uses the terms, the Lover, the Beloved, and the Love between them. A more secular approach would be Hegel's notion of thesis, antithesis and synthesis: there is in each of two distinct things or experiences, a common possibility of connection.

For the Christian faith, this deeper, connecting unity of apparent difference is a force in creation seeking to enable goodness, grace and beauty: the proper 'truth' and fulfilment

for which creation is called into being. But the 'way' is
not of binary analysis and negotiation, but rather it unfolds
through a more spiritual searching for this common life and
wellbeing. What so easily presents as two, is in fact three –
the two different elements or experiences and the common
connector that can emerge: in Augustine's language the Lover,
the Beloved and the Love that joins them. Yet this 'threeness'
or trinity is in fact an organic whole. A simple example
would be the reference that Jesus makes in his teaching to
agricultural imagery – especially parables about the seed and
the soil – 'bits' of life with their own identity and potential,
but only able to develop and flourish by entering into a wider
set of relationships – i.e. with the light which embraces and
enlivens both of them.

The imagery depends upon an already formed creation: the
earth, the ground for his rural hearers. For the theologically
aware the pre-existing reality is the Father, the Creator of
Heaven and Earth.

Within this creation life is born: a seed, or the Son.
A small element with a particular identity and potential.
At the heart of the Gospel is the invitation, in fact the
imperative, for the seed to be placed into the soil, into the
unknown darkness of the soil. This 'way' looks, according
to any wisdom about existence accumulated by immediate
observation, a path to almost certain suffering and death.
Every instinct in a binary assessment would see the soil as
darkness and death – no light, no air. 'Life' would seem
to depend upon remaining 'above the ground'. The irony
is that such a life will be short-lived – for the seed, as for

a human being: even three score years and ten is not much within the possibility of eternity!

And yet, even as a seed or a Son on the surface of the ground, resistant to this challenge, there is 'evidence' that could be noticed of another force at work. For Christians the Holy Spirit brings a penetrative light and warmth that 'rescues' (or saves) the decaying, broken apart seed in the stark tomb of the soil, by connecting with its potential to grow in a new way – not for itself, but towards the light and the warmth, a process through which the seed becomes something else – a new plant.

This result is a new creation: the 'seed' is discarded in the soil and from it emerges a source of life for the world; fruit, nourishment, creating oxygen and forces for life. There has been a Trinitarian dynamic, the two (soil and seed: Creator and Son) joined in and through a third - a spirit calling out further wholeness or holiness in a way which enables the new creation to be a direct expression of this unifying, creative dynamic.

Further, the course of 'life' for the new creation follows the same pattern: the challenge of weeds and inhospitality in the environment, i.e. the complexity of diversity and conflict. This requires struggle to conserve the growth of fruit or flower, but these triumphant expressions of goodness and beauty must succumb to the bigger truth of fading, failing, falling back into the ground. Life begins, continues, ends and begins in ever new ways, within the Trinitarian dynamic of soil, seed, sunshine: of Father, Son and Holy Spirit.

The way that Jesus uses these analogies makes clear that weeds grow out of the soil too. Creation as humanity experiences it is not a perfect 'system', but a testing journey involving choices, challenges and sometimes apparent defeat. Any final 'weeding' and 'harvesting' will come at the end of the age: but the essential process of two becoming three to be joined in one remains central to any proper participation in the instinct to fulfil potential and struggle for different kinds of continuing development. This reality requires, therefore, not just the faith to participate, against many of the insights of the most immediate evidence, but a continuing effort to pay attention, to the soil, to the nature of being a seed, and to the need to challenge and control the continuing menace of weeds. Any gardener knows this reality – the inherent powers in nature to smother or blight what goodness and beauty require in order to flourish and grow in certain ways.

For Christians, to live in the Trinity is to be aware of the complexities of a process that works through two becoming three to become one: while paying attention to the contribution each must make to enable the most fruitful flourishing of the part of the Vineyard in which they are set. Sometimes the 'weeds' are of human making, and sometimes destructive and smothering forces just seem to appear: in each case the reality of the challenge requires the response of faith and a willingness to give the seeds of 'self' into the fullness of the soil, even though available 'evidence' will always identify what seem like less risky possibilities. The fact remains, in nature, as in the fullness of the Christian Gospel, that any response short of self-sacrifice has a very time limited possibility: the frame of human history rather than the glory of eternal life.

Therefore, to live in the Trinity involves paying attention to the weeds, the forces of destruction and alternative 'flourishing', while also looking to notice and celebrate the light and warmth of the sun – the forces of creation, the Word who gives life to every part of creation – a life that in Him can grow into a fullness beyond any human imagining. Further, it is important to notice that the forces of darkness and light keep growing – whether noticed or not by those living in their midst. The common connector is the mystery of the instinct for life, the call to offer that life into an unknown darkness, and the power of the light and warmth that infuses and inhabits every part of creation: the soil, the seed, and the sun: The Father, the Son, the Spirit. In the language of St Augustine: The Lover, the Beloved, and the Love which flows between.

This 'image' has been explored in some depth because history bears witness to the temptation for individuals and for institutions to try to 'capture' their experience of this good news, in a way which ironically atrophies into a vain attempt to 'freeze' the seed they are becoming: to rest in a confidence of belief and behaviour that assumes the 'conquest' of the continuing process of darkness and death: an attempt to set up a colony of heaven on earth. This tendency is understandable, and to some extent, perhaps, inevitable, given the strong instinct to live in the sunshine and keep out inclement weather. Urbanisation witnesses to a growing human capacity to concentrate upon creating a secure and 'weatherproof' home, separated from the signs and rhythms of the natural world.

The problem is highlighted through the powerful theme in the Christian Gospel of the need for human beings to be 'on the way' (hodos). The call to give themselves into a process which calls for living by faith, in an unending movement of complexity and diversity. It is significant that the central act which summarises the teaching of Jesus and is commanded as the key to remembering His Way, is the breaking of the seed, of the bread, in the faith that God gathers fragments to create his glory into eternity. To live in the Trinity demands the courage to live as a fragment, continually reminded of mortality, darkness and destruction, amidst attempts to notice, receive and celebrate the new light of salvation (i.e. full health).

This power of love is a living force that brings hope and transformation, not a settled security in a finished state. Scripture is a story of journeys, often in tents, always beyond fixed places, roles or identities. To live in the Trinity is to live a restless life – where God continues to bless and transform, amidst the reality of weeds, struggle and disappointment. There is a continuing journey: two becomes three becomes one. The container is always a 'covenant': relationships of promise and hope which enable every participant to find appropriate focus and confidence. In the Eucharist the 'new' covenant invites participation in this process of identifying and owning the weeds (within and without), taking the fruits to be destroyed and formed into something else (grains into bread), and each person engaging directly by consuming this offering in an act of destruction that releases the power and light of eternity. The story of Jesus as Son, fulfilling the purposes of the Father in the power of the Spirit: a story whose promise and process every son and daughter is invited to inhabit and celebrate.

Within this dynamic of living in the Trinity, there needs to be careful discernment about seasons – their challenges and opportunities. For any individual, group, church, nation, there will be times for planting, times for waiting, times for combating destructive forces, times for receiving, times for celebrating, times for stepping towards the darkness. The art of seeking spiritual direction, or of offering public worship, involves discerning seasons as appropriate, always within the context of observing the overarching framework of the 'seasons' structured by the Church's year. To live in the Trinity is to live as a particular part, in a particular context.

The key is to resist the superficial attraction of the binary – of seeing ourselves, the world, our possibilities, as 'this' and 'that' – and instead, taking responsibility ourselves for how these different elements are assessed and brought into appropriate relationship. There needs to be space to discern a still, small voice – in each person, in relationships, in nature, that gives light to the overall sense of direction, but also illuminates the path for each individual element. This underlines the fact that public worship and private prayer need to be in the closest relationship. And both need to seek continuing direction, rather than solidify around what might seem to be established methods, practices or answers. The human tendency to capture and close down possibilities in the name of 'control', must learn to pay attention to the continuing effects of warmth and light enabling the emergence of a further new life.

To live in the Trinity will be complex, challenging and always introducing difference: Jesus uses the phrase 'new life'. Given the understandable tendency in a stressful world for many people to come to church seeking some kind of 'rest', the reality they encounter needs to be sensitive and welcoming, but witnessing to the integrity of the journey that the Body of Christ and each of its members must continually explore. To live in the Trinity is to choose to become caught up in the drama of salvation – the opening up of the flesh, or materialness of creation, to the power of goodness and beauty, within, between and beyond each creature.

This explains the centrality of the cross for Christian discipleship: to be a disciple is to follow the way of the cross – as a journeying, not as a one-off moment. The sun somehow reaches the seed in the soil, broken open by forces beyond its control – often through the three days of anxious waiting and apparently imminent failure.

Christians worship before the cross. Discipleship is to follow the Crucified One. In the garden as new life emerged, Mary, highly trained in discipleship, tried to hold on to what she was being offered. There is comfort in control and certainty. But the challenge was to let go of this gift, not to cling on, because the new life is for others too – and for any individual as they remain in search mode. Jesus says 'Do not hold me' – rather let go, and enter into a process, a journey which invites all of humanity. Christians pray so as to be able to recognise and receive the gift, but also to have the courage to step back and make space for others: giving the self into a greater and more mysterious process – the way which is living in the Trinity: the gift of the Father, through the Son, in the all-embracing power of the Spirit.

2

Unity and Diversity

The advantage of binary thinking is that it can help highlight the particular identity of the parts of the world around, and thus clarify differences, enabling work on how best separate elements might relate – on a spectrum from close connection to maintaining distinct identities.

As people seek more tools to discover their own 'identity' there has arisen a need to examine more closely how an ever widening range of 'differences' should be managed. Within this necessary, and often urgent work, there are liberal approaches privileging the primary importance of each autonomous individual, buttressed with rights to ensure being in charge of such a process, as well as more communitarian or socialistic schemes for emphasising the primary importance of various kinds of social relationship (from marriage to ethnicity to political groupings). The outcomes of these competing forces are increasing stress for both 'finding' and 'pursuing' identity.

A more realistic approach is to recognise the reality that alongside the primary binaries of light and dark, male and female, heaven and earth – there are, in between, all kinds of shades, or states of gender, awareness, or readings of soil and sun, experience and aspiration. The reality of created life is one grounded in unevenness: with a very complex degree of possibilities and therefore of perceptions. Hence the sign of the rainbow to collect and signify the range of human hopes and possibilities. There is a spectrum along which people find identities, and sometimes travel in order to do so.

The temptation of Christian theology, aware of the radical inclusivity of the mission of the kingdom pursued by Jesus, is to be drawn towards a simplistic faith that all these differences and complexities are joined up in one great process – so that God is in everyone and everything. This easily becomes a form of pantheism – attractive in its inclusivity, but almost always prone to affirm people and movements 'where they are' rather than demand any radical shifts and changes. An emphasis develops to highlight reconciliation and radical inclusivity: both key ingredients of the Christian Gospel. However, reconciliation and inclusivity can never be sought from the position of secure and settled states: the temptation is to fasten on to 'our' identity – from which any negotiation must take place.

The primary process of living in the Trinity is to enter darkness and the destruction of identity – not simply to defend it self-righteously. There is a salutary parable of a house swept clean, and thus becoming ever more vulnerable to the powers of darkness. That was the failing of established groups such as the Scribes and the Pharisees in the New Testament. There will be 'weeds' within as much as without, and this ongoing reality is highlighted by the emphasis which Jesus places upon pruning, growing, being joined in common roots and a common soil.

And for the Christian disciple, the spiritual life represents a self-conscious attempt to own sin, failure and darkness, and the search for an as yet unrecognisable fullness of life – which comes as gift to be received, not as settlement for human agents to simply negotiate and then capture. The weeds and the wheat grow together, so that this struggle for identity and clarity will always be provisional and subject to revision. All the variety of points on the spectrum have a place, but the key shapers, markers and measures are the pillars of creation from which every variation obtains its bearings and its provisional identity. Hence the foundational significance of a creation narrative that Jesus, in his choice of language and images, clearly endorses and reinforces: light and dark, male and female, heaven and earth...

The cross, at the heart of the Trinity – God calling to God in love, in the midst of the confusions of human identities and the clash of differences (see Psalm 22) – is a sign not just of the reality of the darkness and destruction that clear and hardened identities create, but also of the unevenness which can become the very stuff of salvation – full health. In the darkness and destruction of competing identities muddled in all the confusions of the Passion narratives, the warmth and light of the Spirit continue to call, heal and rise into new life. And in that new life the oneness is not a pantheistic embrace of everyone and every place on every spectrum of differences. Rather, that new life is a gift that enables a gracious receiving of love that celebrates the founding pillars of creation while anticipating their proper reconciliation – in the mercy and the glory of God – not through negotiated human settlements that unwittingly raise up temporary staging posts into permanent defensive positions of self-security.

This whole dynamic plays itself out most explicitly in the crescendo of inclusive and including teaching, climaxing in the gathering of pilgrims, disciples, onlookers and passers-by in the triumphal entry into Jerusalem – followed immediately by the collapse of support and cohesion, the manoeuvring of factions, even within the band of disciples, and the capture, torture and murder of the Messenger of salvation for this whole 'world'. Humanity exposed as incapable of reconciliation and radical inclusivity. Difference always rises to destroy unity in merely 'human' history.

And yet in this very mix identities, failed endeavours (including that of Jesus and His followers), light begins to dawn. The entrance to the tomb of human endeavour and complexity is opened. New life emerges – neither to be captured, nor to endorse any particular place on any of the spectrums. Rather, all these shades are blessed – not in their own self-shaped identities, but as seeds of a new kingdom, where the markers for growth are measured by the needs of others, especially those not yet connected with the invitation. In this new world of salvation, offered in its introductory state, there will no longer be light and dark, but one perpetual light: no longer male or female, but one obedient, worshipping citizenship, no longer heaven and earth, but one abiding city.

But on the way, on this journey – the hodos of Jesus – the invitation is to own living in the Trinity, the will of the Father, the way of the Son, the embrace of the Spirit. Lived amongst weeds and wheat, pursued amidst manifold unevenness, humble not to claim settlement as finished identities. A journey owning the binaries of light and dark, male and female, heaven and earth, but realistic about all the shades in between: sometimes shades of wickedness, and sometimes shades of only seeing through the glass darkly. The journey in the Trinity becomes the study of unevenness: searching for unity as we acknowledge the realities of all the shades of diversity, their potential and their seductive limitations which so easily become presented as finished articles.

Jesus chooses not the high path of perfection, but the lower way of wandering, challenging encounter and frustratingly uneven outcomes. Even the disciples seem to consistently fail to understand, or to act as might be expected from such high quality tutoring and formation. There is no escape into a perfect place, even for diligent disciples. Unity is a spirit which embraces, but also inhabits other, very different elements in creation, in so far as any one person, group or tradition can see. Unity is in diversity – but more, unity embraces through a diversity of elements which are increasingly ready to be dissolved and broken open, to allow new, yet unknown, life to emerge. An interesting sign to church groups locked in combat over issues of identity, inclusion and reconciliation.

The Spirit gives unity through the miracle of sacrifice, the fraction of the seed: not through agreed compromises about

mutual flourishing. The agenda and power belong to God
– gifts to be received. A spirituality often undermined by
personal rules of life and patterns of public worship – both
of which can so easily confuse 'method' with 'answer' and
'evenness' with 'success'.

Yet such a Spirit comes from the will of the Father
into the robust earthiness of the Son: spirit made flesh
amidst darkness and brokenness. A spirituality which cries
from the soul rather than seeks justification for the self.
The difference is crucial and subtle. Too often Christian
conversation in synods and working groups fails to honour
this crucial distinction between soul and self, such is the
power of difference as identity, and unity as a construction
we are continuously called to build.

To live in the Trinity is to take seriously the sheer
earthiness, sensuousness, challengingness and complexity of
trying to be human, open to the Spirit, following the way
of the Cross, to conform to our call to fulfil the will of the
Father.

The question for Christian praying then becomes, not
'how can I better live the higher life of spiritual perfection?',
but 'how can I better risk engaging with the low, fleshly life
that needs to be fully earthed before it can be broken open
and drawn towards heaven?' What might such a perspective
mean for conversation, comparing lifestyles and shades on
the spectrums? To be living in the Trinity more consciously
is to be committed to receiving grace in these challenging
complexities – rather than through sorting them out. We

do have to prepare, plough and plant the soil – but all these necessary endeavours will always be subject to the weather - that is forces beyond our control, as well as being affected by the strengths and weaknesses of our own efforts. Further, all these endeavours and forces unfold within the all-pervading warmth and light of God's continuing presence and purposes.

To be a Christian disciple is to be part of a Body, with one Head, but many different parts, including those that some would judge to be unseemly. The part each plays is not for its own wellbeing and particular identity – but to contribute humbly to a life beyond the comprehension of any one contributing component.

The task of the church as an institution is to find ways of expressing and organising these realities – of presence and purpose, of parts and partialities. While other institutions strive to give people clarity, identity, security and insurance against unevenness, the church invites into a space for 'sinners' – those who know the unevenness of life, and plunge into it, at cost to their own identities, in order to make witness to a different order of unity and connection.

In the powerful world of Google and effective management there are 'answers' - which are often helpful and encouraging. But these proper endeavours need to be held within a different environment, which celebrates different parts and perspectives, while encouraging each to own their penultimacy, their need for greater vision, and their tendency to settle rather than journey. The church will always be an institution which works through chaos in merely human terms, yet in the divine economy of the Trinity there is, unavoidably, a place for the sword as the way to peace. The piercing of Jesus' side is the sign of reality for the church as an agent of unity amidst diversity. The way will be messy, tragic, full of serious misunderstandings and harmful actions – yet held in the Spirit of healing grace and life-giving hope.

And for any member of the church, the first steps always involve removing the mote from their own eye. Prayer asks for darkness to be dispelled, and for light to shine: the journey stays rooted in fallen identities ever called to give themselves into the process of the destruction which leads to blessing. The outcomes in practical terms can never be anticipated in detail. That is why the Church is called to be a spiritual institution rooted in the mess and chaos of the lower roads of human endeavour. Mary provides the summary 'Behold, the handmaid of the Lord', and thereby giving herself into greater purposes than she might ever understand or oversee. The ego gives way to the invitation of the Holy Spirit. Famous examples would be Teresa of Avila and St John of the Cross – both of whom were part of the Reformation in the Roman Catholic Church in Spain in the sixteenth century. They each joined religious orders, but felt that existing arrangements had become too 'comfortable' and needed reform to emphasise the radical nature and witness of the Gospel. For both 'reformers', their attempt to look at the motes in their own eyes, led to persecution from other members of their order, who wanted to defend the 'perfections' already achieved through their institutional arrangements. Too often disciples find rest in

a church of settlement. Jesus brought a similar challenge to
the highly organised and genuinely devout religious 'orders'
of his own time.

St. John was kidnapped by members of his own order
and imprisoned in a small shed for nine months. In the
darkness, and lacking proper nourishment, St. John created
one of the world's great spiritual poems – a source of light
for the world from the darkness of a tomb constructed by
human differences.[1] A gift of unity in the Holy Spirit amidst
the cruel manifestations of diversity pursued through more
traditional human approaches to organisation as answer and
finished product. The poetry of praise amidst the prose of
institutional coherence. The high roads of Christian ordering
and achievement will always need challenging in the light of
owning the realities of the lower roads of chaos and confusion
– so that they too can be embraced in the oneness of the life
of the Trinity.

Flowers bloom, but always fade, and then fall. But living
goes on – always new and yet always within recognisable
parameters.

---

[1] The Spiritual Canticle.

3

Participation

Invitation to the Party

Living in the Trinity is participating in the flow of creation, not adhering to particular doctrines or patterns of behaviour. And creation has a rhythm – the triumph of light over darkness. Human beings emerge into this flow and this rhythm, but soon imbibe a tendency to build islands of resistance – settlements over against these basic dynamisms.

Religion can easily become a form of constructing the most subtle and sophisticated islands of resistance. To counter these temptations towards honing institutional solidarity and cohesion, Archbishop Rowan Williams redefined mission as 'noticing what God is doing and joining in'. Otherwise the Trinity will become relegated to the arena of 'doctrine' and disconnected from the fuller gift which the church so deeply needs in order to be continually receiving new life.

Living in the Trinity involves engaging in the flow of creation that continually creates change, new experiences, different challenges, disturbing possibilities. A wonderful invocation of this invitation is offered in Psalm 19. The heavens declare the glory of God – the continuing sign in nature, of light and warmth amidst the complexities of creation: the sun rises across creation; nothing is hidden from its heat. The dynamism of nature. Then the Psalmist points to 'The law of Lord, perfect in reviving the soul'. God's word and witness "make wise the simple... and rejoices the heart". There is dynamism from engaging with the teaching and tradition of the church: no chance to rest in settled beliefs or behaviours. These dynamic forces in creation and the Law of the Lord bring warnings to those who engage – a call to own sinfulness and failures – a need for forgiveness. Only then, having become open to finding one's place in creation, can the disciple be equipped and enabled to seek others in their discernment and response. There are to be no islands of resistance – just bold walking with others, including towards the inevitability of the darkness which seems to herald destruction.

This deep spiritual truth is safeguarded by the church making baptism the foundation of a more fully committed Christian life: a discipline of seeking cleansing, renewal and refreshment. The way of confession and absolution: the method of being plunged into the waters of salvation to be blessed more fully by the Holy Spirit. This common and continuing spiritual root enables a deep connectivity despite the apparent differences between the plants and the fruits the various seeds seem to produce. The tasks can shift from comparing and evaluating the 'fruits', to seeking to explore the commonness of the soil and the sun. Then participation in the process of creation becomes the basis for exploring connection and co-operation. Differences in expression or flavour become less definitive in any evaluation of diversity. Jesus provided the image of the vine, or the sower, to emphasise this important point. Participation in the flow of creation results from the gift of a life, a call, a path of possibility. Christ creates the seed (the light that lightens every person (John 1 [1-14]) and Christ gathers the fruits – though not without discernment. Fruit or fish 'rejected' go back into the processes of creation.

In the same way the sacraments offer this participation in the processes of creation to all – but remain available for those who at any particular moment seem to reject them. Baptism, Eucharist, confession – remain moments to enrich every person, and will always be the foundation of an invitation to come and clarify what God might be doing in human lives to enable a more profound participation in His very own life of the Trinity, through being given the breath of existence: the call to each person is to recognise and this receive this gift more fully.

This is a radically inclusive gospel, designed to overthrow islands of resistance and stable settlement, in favour of owning common roots and goals – albeit by differing paths.

This radical inclusivity calls the church to always have open and porous boundaries, and her workings to be spaces of learning through the Trinitarian process of separating, breaking and healing that Baptism and Eucharist highlight. The salient point is that the church can never be measured by performance, since this will always reflect the unevenness and fearfulness of creaturely life. Performance is a way of measuring oneself, based upon available and identifiable data.

By contrast, the church must always be measured by her vision – to be nourished and enacted while on the 'way'. Vision can never be narrowly analysed or expressed: it needs poetry rather than prose: liturgy rather than ordinary language. The impetus is towards and beyond, an embracing of a not yet that approaches laden with promise. This is the spirit of the Beatitudes, when Jesus teaches His disciples and the crowds. This is a common currency – the instinct in the human heart to value and seek justice, peace, common fulfilment, amidst the tendencies towards riches, satisfaction, and separateness. Blessings and woes can be recognised through a universal register: things to be pursued and things to be avoided.

In practical terms these perspectives imply that participation in the life of the Trinity, the path of discipleship which is willing to carry a cross, will not necessarily mean joining the church as an institution. Rather the test and the route will more clearly involve participation in the projects which enable the flow of creation to better spread across the complexities and defensiveness of so many of God's children and the journeys they are trying to craft.

Hence Baptism and Eucharist will never be simply to define and nourish members of the church as an organised body. This important work will always need to be tested by the vision and the outreach of the practical projects being pursued across the wide diversities of human endeavours and conflicts. The challenge is to disciple people into projects which need the refinement and empowering of word and sacrament, rather than simply training people for more committed membership limited to a merely liturgical expression.

The call is to make a difference in God's world in respect of playing a part to facilitate the flow of grace and the welcoming warmth and light of the Holy Spirit. But although every creature is a participant through invitation, there needs to be a vision and a witness through particular projects – to give the focus and the signs which the 'world' needs. Projects can give focus to vision, to enable meaningful participation as a proper expression of baptised Eucharistic life within the wider world.

Perhaps the most distinctive picture of a project which Jesus offers is that of a party. While other religious leaders and groups had laws, constitutions and firm frameworks, Jesus invited all kinds of people into a very open social space – with food and drink as the key to acting out the sharing and social connection that best allows the flow of grace and goodness. There were organised parties such as the Wedding at Cana, impromptu parties such as the feeding of the five-thousand or the welcoming of Matthew, and the joining of other people's parties, such as that of Simon the Pharisee.

Parties enable a special space for participation. There is a 'theme' that gives permission for gathering, but space for varying degrees of engagement. Thus some may be called up higher, or a woman of the town participate while held by some to be an outsider. Food and drink connect people in the basic being of humanness, whether kings holding feasts or Jesus trying to gather and encourage His followers and the publicans and prostitutes attracted to them.

Yet participation goes deeper. "I am the bread" – there is a presence in the seeds of creation that can be recognised and welcomed. There can be a sharing in substance without needing to name or own differences. In one parable the king compels people to come: different agendas should be no excuse.

Such participation is in a spirit which the party offers, celebrates and shares amongst those willing to join. The aim is to enjoy both the 'theme' and each other – whatever more private differences or particular reservations participants might harbour. The defining 'party' of the Last Supper created a sharing which involved Peter and Judas (Jesus' betrayers) and all those who were to run away and abandon him. Yet the connection they had shared in His presence and power was not only to endure, but to continue to nourish and encourage.

The fact that there are subgroups and less public conversations adds to the riches of the texture of this particular form of participation – not least because of the common ownership of an inclusive atmosphere and an openness to new things. Parties enable strangers to become friends – not through negotiation of differences, but by sharing food, drink and a trust in that human generosity which gives the confidence to be alongside others with goodwill and graciousness.

In this sense a party allows participation in an atmosphere where there can be visitation – by others, and by a common, connecting Spirit of greater wholeness and hope. This can operate even if some participants are unsure about being present, or nervous of others.

The Trinity is an invitation to a party – the kind of open, generous, forgiving, unifying hospitality that God offers in the Eucharist. To live in the life of the Trinity is to be at a party. Even a character as dissolute and self-centred as the Prodigal Son, no doubt organising parties simply for his own benefit, discovers when he seeks help from his family, that the Father offers neither a judgement nor therapy – but simply a party. A context within which all these complexities can be embraced positively for those with the courage to attend. A dissolving goodness reconnected the Prodigal despite the many barriers his behaviour had created. And the refusal of his elder brother to attend illustrates that the party of life in the Trinity is always an invitation that can be ignored or rejected. The Prodigal, whose life had become fractured and destroyed through constructing his own island of resistance, with no prospect of bearing much fruit, simply had to step into the party which celebrated the mysterious power of resurrection: He was dead and is now alive.

Of course, to have parties does not solve people's problems, but it enables a richer kind of perspective and vision to be tasted. To live in the Trinity is to be drawn into these risky, extraordinary, loving relationships, which can be touched by the good news of resurrection. That is the agenda for any party.

By contrast, there is a tendency to highlight 'issues' and magnify the struggle. This becomes a subtle way of putting self at the centre. The love of the Trinity is unconditional in invitation, in hopefulness and in new possibilities which could emerge – both in terms of perspectives and relationships. The key is not solving problems, but opening hearts to common grounds and gracious being together.

And a party eventually ends. What people do with the experience disappears from view – back into separate and differentiated existences. The party highlights the importance of sacraments – moments which offer direction, formation and inclusive hopefulness. St John explores the workings of the light which lightens every creature, through reporting a series of moments – signs. Mostly through the gathering of unusual 'parties'. The sign to set the scene is the Wedding at Cana. A wedding is a party for people who do not know each other through established relationships, to come together and begin to build some kind of common bond. Drink is an important fuel to lighten inhibitions and provide a happy confidence. The best known human efforts failed to provide enough drink: Jesus created a huge amount of high quality wine – a radical investment in parties being the way of participation which is rich, realistic, and captured in a moment that will unfold through all the freedoms that each of the participants rightly claim in living their everyday life. There needs to be structure: a master of ceremonies, etiquette about serving food and drink – but there also needs to be freedom for the Spirit to embrace and connect.

A party is a sign, a moment which gives particular focus to the flow of creation, and then allows participants to remain in charge of what they choose to receive. But grace is offered, and generally tasted to some degree. Living in the Trinity by pitching up to a party. Not a message widely offered by our churches!

4

Creed

Believing is Belonging

The two great creeds of the Christian Church offer an invitation into the life of the Trinity. For many people the creeds have a long history of being documents to be discussed and disputed. Often they are marginalised as being the product of a different culture and way of thinking.

Of course the creeds are not statements to be understood, or given intellectual assent. They are narratives produced for worship – prayers. Creeds are part of the process of putting ourselves into the presence of God, within the living story of His power and His purposes. They are gifts to those who turn to God in prayer. Thus the creeds are part of the flow of God's life into creation – designed to colonise us, not to be colonised by human attempts to measure and judge by the current intellectual standards of any particular age. Creeds begin with the statement I/we believe: not understand. To say the creed is not an expression of a particular understanding of God: it is to put oneself into the life of the Trinity.

The nineteenth century Anglican theologian F.D. Maurice argued that the creeds safeguarded the freedom of Christians to know and love God whatever the intellectual fashions amongst the clergy for interpreting and explaining them. They pointed to a deeper area of connection and spiritual wellbeing.

Similarly Charles Gore, who was the Bishop of Oxford at the beginning of the twentieth century, was keen to distinguish between the responsibilities of the ordained, ministerial priesthood, to teach and explore an orthodox faith consistent with scripture and the recognised teaching of the church, and the freedom of the laity to pursue their discipleship within the much less detailed or simply indicative frame of the creeds – which allowed a necessary and important variety of experience and expression, appropriate for the mysterious diversity of views and values that God seems to raise up among His people.

The Nicene Creed gives a certain amount of detail around a Trinitarian structure. It was the product of considerable wrestling by the leaders of the Early Church. The indications of the life of the Trinity are embroidered with further details. For instance the affirmation "I believe in one God, the Father Almighty" is followed by "Maker of heaven and earth, of all things visible and invisible". Similarly regarding Jesus Christ – "the only-begotten Son of God, begotten of the Father before all worlds, God of God, Light of Light, very God of God; begotten not made, being of one substance with the Father, by whom all things were made." Further this creed proclaims "And I believe in the Holy Ghost, the Lord and

Giver of Life; who proceeds from the Father (and the Son); who with the Father and the Son together is worshipped and glorified."

This is a creed which places the story of the Trinity within a more detailed frame of reference. It naturally leads to further questioning and exploration.

There is a more simple and direct focus in the Apostle's Creed, which is more directly a prayer and a very simple narrative. There are three short paragraphs: three persons: God as Trinity.

I believe in God, the Father almighty
creator of heaven and earth.

I believe in Jesus Christ, his only Son, our Lord,
who was conceived by the Holy Spirit,
born of the Virgin Mary,
suffered under Pontius Pilate,
was crucified, died, and was buried,
he descended to the dead.
On the third day he rose again;
he ascended into heaven,
he is seated at the right hand of the Father,
and he will come to judge the living and the dead.

I believe in the Holy Spirit,
the holy Catholic Church,
the communion of saints:
the forgiveness of sins,

the resurrection of the body:
and the life everlasting.
Amen.

This is a prayer – an opportunity to enter a process and to experience the dynamics of life in the Trinity.

The first paragraph places trust in God as Father, as Almighty and as Creator of all that we can conceive: heaven and earth. It begins at the highest possible point. God as power, purpose and yet parental: majesty and yet intimacy. The possibility of relationship into the ultimate, and yet through the everyday. This is a prayer seeking connection with the fullness and fulfilment of creation: and yet with recognition of the soil of life with all its mysterious challenges and potential. The prayer begins in glory, in perfection, in the fullness of creation.

The second paragraph – "I believe in Jesus Christ, His only Son, our Lord" brings us lower down. Our Lord, Model, Saviour, is one with God the Father. Yet born of the Virgin Mary, though conceived by the Holy Spirit – a mixing of flesh and spirit: divinity and humanity. The context is closer to ourselves. The human is becoming more prominent as we lower our sights within the narrative of this prayer.

Suffered under Pontius Pilate. The aspiration for goodness and glory is challenged by islands of resistance, defending narrower ideas and values. He was crucified, dead, and buried – plunged into the darkness of the earth: apparently destroyed by death. The trajectory brings us lower – from God, to goodness, to conflict within human affairs, to depravity and evil seeming to gain the upper hand, and finally to the darkness of death. The creed takes us on a journey from the glory of God to the frailty and mortality of human fleshliness. A journey every human being can recognise and which will, to an extent, include us all. He descended into hell.

On the third day – that is in God's time, requiring a period of human waiting and attention – He rose again. Being plunged into the darkness of the ground, to be broken open, was not the end, but a different kind of beginning. Only from such a depth, and as the result of an unremitting downward journey, can there be the spiritual formation through which humanity can be truly raised upward – in the direction of where God dwells in the fullness of his majesty.

He rose again and he ascended into heaven – rising out of the earth towards the true light and warmth of the Creator. He is seated at the right hand of the Father. – raised up to the highest heaven. His journey of decent to the depths and then being raised up to the highest place, is of course the journey for every Christian prayer and every created person.

The way involves an inevitability of suffering and death and an attitude of self-sacrifice into what the world assumes to be darkness and simply death. This lowest point in worldly eyes is in fact the gate of resurrection.

From where he will come to judge the living and the dead – by the standards and contours of participation in this journey – from highest aspiration, through the lowest depths of darkness, to the way into eternity. The key is judgement of the whole of each life. The unfolding of human engagement within this journey from heights to depths is the way of finding true resurrection and eternal life. This is the journey in the Father, through the way of the Son.

Then the Apostle's Creed celebrates the power and purpose coursing through this everlasting process – "I believe in the Holy Spirit". Through the Holy Spirit unfold the tools and markers for this journey of human being. The holy Catholic Church is the clearest manifestation of the Body of Christ as it experiences and struggles to follow the path of discipleship. 'Catholic' is a term which ensures the inclusive universality of the church's structures and sacraments. Anything less will succumb to the temptation to become as island of resistance – a more limited endeavour which will only flourish at the expense of others. The life of the Trinity flows through the whole of creation, inviting recognition, reception and rejoicing.

The power of the Holy Spirit also embraces the Communion of Saints – all those who have gone before, and who are yet to come. The radical inclusivity of all creation throughout time and space.

Then the register changes, from the inclusivity of the project to the power that enables its fulfilment "I believe... in the forgiveness of sins". The core of the Good News in Jesus the Son is ownership of the realities of human fallenness – the plethora of islands of resistance – and yet the possibility that grace can raise sights to a greater aspiration, while providing the only means for making this transition – the forgiveness of sins – recovery from missing the mark and falling short.

Forgiveness enables facing of the darkness and a confidence of growing through such a painful ownership of culpability into a person healed, restored and renewed. The dynamic of baptism, eucharist and confession.

Free grace is the food of the resurrection of the body: the miracle that the very site and source of sin, human fleshliness (especially as identified by St Paul) can be renewed: re-membered in the words of the eucharist. And, of course, the body is a sign of the connectivity of all flesh in its potential to contribute to the proper flourishing of the resurrection process.

In his own Resurrection Jesus bears the marks of the conflict and divisions in His flesh. An amazing sign that each of us, in our weakness and vulnerabilities is nonetheless the stuff of resurrection: not because of something inherent in the fleshliness, but because of the indwelling gift and power of the Holy Spirit – the indwelling of the life of the Trinity in all its life giving mystery.

Some religions focus upon the soul, as a faculty to be detached and freed from the body. This kind of dualism often leads to the denigration of material existence: in terms of our earlier analogy, soil and seeds are discarded: all focuses on a separated, superior, spiritual world and existence. The glory of the Christian Gospel, unveiled through the Trinity, is that every part of creation is called to contribute, with human beings called to a particular priestly ministry of mediating grace to encourage reception of this precious gift of Life.

Human beings, in all our sinfulness, brokenness, incompleteness, through the crucified and risen Christ, can be drawn into a resurrection of the Body which is Life everlasting. This is the glorious vision of the Book of Revelation – people joined in a common life as citizens together of the city of God. Structures and systems are still important.

In this way the Apostle's Creed is an invitation to pray into the life of the Trinity. It outlines the power and process of God, the relationships and structures through which each person can be embraced into this life-giving mystery. This story is to be recognised, embraced and inhabited through the daily praying of the Apostle's Creed. Such prayerfulness will illuminate and empower the structures to hold us through the journey in an ordered whole. The key is holiness. The simplest early Christian creed was "Holy, Holy, Holy": the wholeness of Father, Son and Spirit to order humanity into an inclusive Body, able to recognise and recover from sin, and nourished by the power which connects, enlightens and embraces into eternity.

Our more immediate task is to allow this whole-making spirit of salvation to be active in our everyday relationships and endeavours: opening up potentially divisive issues of identity and difference, not to a measurable resolution, but into an atmosphere of graciousness. Hope directed towards God and the fulfilment of His mission, rather than aspirations shaped by more human, immediate concerns and experiences.

Praying the creed provides shape and direction for becoming a community of saints, the Body of Christ fulfilling its proper calling. The Gospel of St John uses the terms

'Advocate' and 'Comforter' for the Holy Spirit – these are the precise needs in human being which the Trinity meets: comfort in the struggles with fallen, sinful human endeavours, and advocacy of a better path, manifest in the gift of the Father and the way of the Son, a power and presence enabling and pursuing wholeness.

The Apostle's Creed is the frame for our life journey; our death journey; our resurrection journey. A journey to be enacted daily amidst the challenges of complexity, diversity and disappointment.

5

Personal

Throughout history there has been considerable debate about the 'persons' of the Trinity. Person is a category that denotes capacity for relationship – rather than simply a body or an automaton. In the personal there is potential for exploration, differences that might expand or converge, and a reflective ability to assess and adjust. Just as it is possible to see these elements in human beings within the context of nature, so such characteristics can give intimations of deeper and more eternal registers – not least the primary experiences of faith, hope and love. Hence an indication of an echo of the nature of the Creator, the purpose of the creation, and the power which enables its most fruitful unfolding. This framework has been long established as a way of approaching the mystery of the Trinity.

In more recent times, particularly after Charles Darwin, there has been highlighted the idea of evolution, driven by the possibilities of development and improvement. This was amusingly captured in a famous nineteenth century cartoon depicting a steady progression from slime to apes to a bowler hatted Victorian gentleman, the crown of creation. Such a scheme of improvement for civilisations as much as for individuals, has become quite commonplace - despite considerable evidence of serious setbacks and dysfunction, whether through natural disasters, the enduring nature of human wickedness and violence, or the sheer instability of much that passes for personal relationships.

Fifteen years before Darwin published the Origin of Species; Newman produced an Essay on the Development of Doctrine, which recognised the privileged place of the church in receiving revelation and tools for discernment - thus proving a controlling framework for both the blessings of new life and the disruptions of over-confident schemes and ideas. This was an attempt to measure and evaluate progress within an already given frame of Christian doctrine: though allowing for development of church teaching consistent with a number of already established controlling markers.

Both Darwin's theory of evolution, and Newman's Doctrine of Development, too easily assumed an ability to identify, communicate and evaluate any impetus towards change and new practices or insights. Their approaches both offer useful tools but do not do justice to the complexities and often apparent contradictoriness of human interaction and the aspiration for growth and improvement.

The concern of both Darwin and Newman was for dependable reference points. The church may sometimes offer authoritative teaching to provide guidance, or a sense of direction, regarding new possibilities arising from the 'progress' of medical science or technological capabilities. The continuing presupposition is of a steady progression, and this prevailing atmosphere subtly persuades Christians that the point of spiritual life and the journey of discipleship should be some kind of steady progress too. Much of church life colludes with this pressure, and serves to add to stress and an unrealistic emphasis upon measurables and outcomes.

However the deeper reality of living in the Trinity, as persons made for all the complexities and challenges of relationships, is to own a tension between the aspiration to be drawn up into the perfection of the Father, the fullness of the Holy Spirit - when in fact, much of our endeavour is marked by the 'fallen' selfishness and short-sightedness that surrounded the journey of Jesus, including institutionalised violence and the apparent triumph of 'evil'. Personhood indicates the dynamics within the Trinity that can embrace and minister to this mysterious and deeply frustrating reality as it continues to bring temptation, sin, tastes of glory and the mood swings of struggle and perseverance: despair and hope: abandonment and love.

Personal relationships need to unfold in the dynamic between knowing and not-knowing – the space where prayer rises ever in the human heart, to seek help or to celebrate and say thanks for blessings. There is a call to trust that by living more self-consciously in this flow of creation it becomes possible to pursue progress, to accept reverses, and to recognise that any human contribution can only be of effect if joined to the greater purposes of the fulfilment of creation in the mysterious tensions between light and dark.

Modern confidence in scientific approaches can tend to emphasise human capacity to learn to understand and shape ourselves and the world within which we are set: sovereignty becomes a real human aspiration. For much of history there has been a stronger acknowledgment of how much in life seems unpredictable or uncomfortable, and thus a clearer turn towards the sovereignty of God and the dominant reality of living with unevenness, particularly in the tensions between seeking fruitful growth while accepting the inevitability of weeds and destruction. There can be a sense of direction but not detailed planning of the route. Thus the 'way' is a journey into the unknown, needing faith as much as a sense of predictable facts and outcomes.

The personal is being aware of the uncertainty always present amidst the conviction of being connected to goodness, hope and glory. Love is the currency of the personal – the energy that enables and celebrates such blessings, while containing the capacity to hold on through disappointments or disasters.

The task of the church becomes to hold the remembrance of blessing, to minister moments and narratives that help provide access to such gracious love, and yet be realistic and supportive through the continuing struggles with sin and darkness. Praying the creed keeps the disciple within this unevenness – seeking the summits of perfection, being drawn down to the depths, yet trusting in the enduring presence and power of new life.

In a time when there is an awareness of issues around
'mental health', this reality of the personal being a work
in progress, like a carving subject to polishing and further
reshaping, sanding or moulding, is an important element to
take seriously. To be a person is to live in a dynamic of the
spiritual – not just the material or the psychological when
understood as a science.

Further there may be an urgent need to recognise
the significance of issues around the 'mental health' of
communities. The confidence in therapy to stabilise and grow
self-aware persons is often replicated in parallel endeavours
to assume the possibility of creating and organising equally
stable and well-ordered groupings of persons – families, work
places, institutions, nations. The result can be unrealistic
expectations and frustration at unfulfilled ideals. There is
a key witness for the Gospel to point to the unevenness of
'community' living, and the magnification of pressures due
to the added variety of 'personal' identities and aspirations.

Jesus was blunt in reminding his followers about the
fragilities and fractures in family life, and the tensions
inevitable in religious and political groupings. This reality
was still a cause for hope, because the personal ingredients
could together be encouraged to live in the life of the Trinity,
and to hold hopes and fears within the prayerful process of
the creed.

Disappointments and dysfunction are not just disasters
to be remedied, but reminders that we live in a world of
competing persons and often apparently incompatible agendas.
Our response needs to be not just practical by way of attempted

repair, but prayerful and humble to recognise the rhythm of
rise and fall through which the grace of salvation emerges.

At the end of the Gospel of Matthew, in a summation
of his teaching, Jesus tells His disciples to go "to teach all
nations", that is community groups or ethne, "baptising them
in the name of the Father, the Son, and of the Holy Spirit".
Through this process he concludes: "and, lo, I am with you
always," – the enduring presence of the life of the Trinity.

St. Paul reaffirms this meaning in the second letter to the
Corinthians: 'the grace of the Lord Jesus Christ, the love and
God and fellowship of the Holy Spirit'. The Christian life
calls persons to be baptised into this ecology, and to continue
to live by being blessed through it.

Unlike the triads of Plato and numerous thinkers since,
this Trinity is not a formula but a set of living relations,
broken down through the Gospel revelation into soil, seed
and sun: that is Creator, creation called to redemption, and
energising power and presence.

The implication of this wisdom is that by living in the
Trinity, each person, by being made in the image of God, is a
little trinity – a complex of these forces giving life, reforming
life and renewing life. Thus, the spiritual journey of each
person can recognise the reality of being created – matter or
material, but with potential. The journey will be uneven,
into the diversities and complexities of light struggling with
darkness. Often outcomes will seem uncertain and sometimes
despairing. Yet, there is a continuing light and warmth

drawing each person through the valley of the shadow of death towards the green pastures of eternity.

Prayer will be exploring this variety of callings, being prepared to acknowledge being placed within a particular place within the rising and falling and renewing of the creedal process. The more personal prayer can acknowledge the importance of discerning moments within these processes, and then summon the courage to seek, while accepting the mystery of God's timing and testing, the richer can be the reception of grace. Jesus was able to cry out in despair on the cross, and in that prayer there was the assurance of presence and possibilities.

Each person needs space to explore particular contexts, and to trust in the power of the Spirit to redeem and raise up. This is a spirituality that shatters the inclination to retreat into the defended territories of the islands of resistance which we are tempted to construct as a misguided way of preserving and protecting the personal. To live in the Trinity is in a sense to be the Trinity, connecting the personal as being, with the personal as becoming, through the personal as blessing. The personal operates in each of these contexts, and thrives by connecting this complex of callings, while acknowledging an essential dependence upon others, and upon the Giver of Grace who invites every person to pursue this path towards glory.

For St Paul the process of a personal life therefore issued in social manifestations, qualities such as being peaceful, patient, forgiving.

Such an understanding of the personal as the means of sharing in the life of the Trinity was in stark contrast to the Greek and Roman emphasis upon the vocation of each person as being to accumulate the means to ensure their own fulfilment, even at the expense of others. Connection was managed through political or social arrangements designed to best protect and enhance persons as individuals. There was little desire to realise a fuller understanding of the personal as relationship in terms of giving the self into the service of the most inclusive community of the kingdom – personhood found by being lost in a greater reality. In this way society flourishes as a "network of realised personalities"[1] – that is societies should become persons being realised in relationships which reflected living in the life of the Trinity.

---

[1] J.R. Illingworth: The Doctrine of the Trinity. Macmillan 1907, p.245.

6

Trinity and Tradition

The Party Plan

The creeds were shaped by the wisdom given to the Church Fathers in the first four centuries. They were challenged to provide a coherent focus for Christian faith in a context where Greek, Roman and pagan forces offered tools for this task in ways which seriously threatened the depth and universality of the Gospel of One who came to bring salvation to the world.

In the conditions in which these foundations for Christian believing were formed, there were many pagan cults, based upon esoteric rituals and a localised, particular understanding of deity closely related to the interests of the worshippers. By contrast, Greek and Roman philosophy had developed sophisticated tools to examine human experience and provide plausible models for comprehensive understanding and future development. From this 'wisdom' emerged models for political organisation and spiritual reflection that could be seen to fit with human experience and aspirations.

The Early Church Fathers were well versed in this world-affirming wisdom, and in the ways of worship that brought comfort and hope to many pagan spiritualities. Nonetheless, they recognised that the foundation of the Gospel revelation was not human experience and it's shaping – but the sheer gift of grace in Christ. This gift provided the means of evaluating and transforming established wisdom and ways of worship.

The Fathers recognised that the gift of grace came through the life of the Trinity, which embraced but also exposed the limitations and fallenness of the human condition. Hence the creedal journey of prayer from heights to depths and then through resurrection into the wholeness given only in the Spirit. Human experience and achievement needs to be handled through this unique power of the Trinity, which refines as it renews.

To explore the implications of this truth of the Gospel, it is important to look at the Last Supper, where Jesus draws together the threads of His teaching and witness in an enacting of how grace can be received. And, of course, the Last Supper is part of a whole pattern of 'parties' – Jesus gathering people for a fellowship which transformed diversity through a taste of a common moment and experience. Moreover the Eucharist was developed by the early church to help participants to recognise this process and to place themselves more self-consciously within it. In this way participation in the Eucharist provided a model of how to engage in other human groupings and encounters. The image of 'party' is important because it indicates a free flow of possibilities, which inevitably include joys as well as engagement and disappointment.

Thus, in the upper room the 'celebration' involved looking forward with confidence and hope in the company of Jesus the Saviour, as well as a huge variety of emotions as Judas prepared for his betrayal and Peter protested strongly about being 'washed' – in a manner that clearly indicates the fragilities he was later to display. To be invited into such a complex fellowship meets with a degree of resistance from the more immediate agendas and experiences of those who seem to have accepted the invitation. This is the challenge that the creedal dynamic seeks to keep in place, and also to offer re-assurance in terms of nourishing the commitment to enter into this process.

The Eucharist therefore offers a 'party plan' which can be a template for all human encounters. The plan explores in more detail the creedal journey.

First comes the willingness to seek the lowest place. The way of Christ from highest heaven through the 'experience' of being born into human fleshliness, to the testing and judgement of Pilate (systems attuned solely to the norms discerned from human experience), to the darkness of torture and death. A call to rise again comes through the gift of God – it is beyond any human capacity to offer or deliver. To seek the lowest place is to accept human limitation and imperfection, not only in the self, but equally in the systems of organisation and exploration which so easily claim the allegiance of creatures confronted by the challenges and complexities of life.

Much human effort is directed towards how best to 'present' in the parties or situations we attend. Jeetendr Sehdev has written a provocative book entitled *The Kim Kardashian Principle*,[1] showing how technology is allowing and encouraging younger generations especially, to present themselves to be 'seen': a SELFIE approach to life, which provides the container for creating and evaluating human experience. Insecurity and the inner knowledge of our imperfection pushes us towards a strategy of self-preservation in which the 'I' is always at the centre of the picture. This tendency is simply a contemporary manifestation of a deep human instinct for preservation and identity.

But when Jesus goes to 'parties' and gatherings, in homes, on the beach, in the wilderness, he notices those usually unnoticed: a leper; a woman suffering from loss of blood; the boy with a few loaves and fishes. The focus and possibilities within human gatherings need to change. One of the reasons for the flourishing of Modern Slavery is that a SELFIE world rarely notices those out of the 'picture' which the self is striving to create.[2]

To live in the Trinity is to recognise the centrality of accepting and following a call to be drawn towards the lowest place – on the edge of established systems, pictures and philosophies. To be decentred is to be open to knowing a need of grace beyond the most immediate and apparently

---

[1] Jeetendr Sehdev. The Kim Kardashian Principle. Little Brown 2017.

[2] Alastair Redfern. The Clewer Initiative. ISPCK 2017.

controllable resources that we tend to accumulate and develop. Only if we can learn to place ourselves in the creed's descent, can we be open to God's call to come up higher.

The resources for this journey, as we descend, and to enable ascent, are not smart human achievements of systems of comfort - but simply the ordinary stuff of creation: the wheat and the vine. That is, the most basic and common ingredients of daily life, available to everybody. Such 'ordinary' elements would seem to need supplementing by human ingenuity and innovation. In fact, these God-given skills very quickly become tools for shaping the world in our own image, because they are immediately developed to build up. To descend is counter intuitive to human attempts to thrive and make sense of life. This tendency needs to be plunged into the more mysterious life of the Trinity, and thus take a more risky and refining route.

Bread and wine emerge not just from human efforts, but from all the vagaries of the weather, the soil - the complex, uncontrollable mysteries of creation.

The third guide from the model of the Last Supper as a feature of the party plan for salvation, is the fact that Jesus reminds those assembled of the narrative of the Passover, the journey of the Salvation of the People, through the creedal process of the highest call, and the long struggle of waiting and wilderness. We need to develop a particular relationship to the stuff of creation - ourselves as well as our subsistence - which owns dependency and the need for grace because of the serious inadequacies of our own efforts - both of achievement and of understanding. Our journey is a part of the calling of all of God's children, within which there is an essential solidarity in the face of the unevenness which recurs.

Fourth, the Eucharist operates through human co-operation with God's calling and gifting. The president holds up the elements and reminds the assembly: "the fruit of the vine, the work of human hands, it will become our spiritual drink". Nature, human endeavour and the transforming gift of divine grace all combined to offer appropriate nourishment for the party – the gathering to accept and pursue vocation into the process of life in the Trinity. Yet our liturgical response is to own that "Lord, we are not worthy", even to be pulled down to the depths, except in the company of Jesus Christ Our Lord. In Romans 8, St. Paul describes the whole of creation struggling with such unworthiness, as opening up the conditions within which wholeness can be given.

In St John's version of the Party, there is the washing of feet – a sign of accepting humbly this need for cleansing and the gifting of grace: it is instructive that the 'leader' of the group, St. Peter, is least equipped to simply receive and thus participate in this way: he is too confident in his own understanding and judgement. This is the danger for all committed Christian people: humility becomes disconnected from the most basic dependencies, and instead becomes a frame for a self-centred identity.

The heart of the Party is the prayer of consecration and blessing – Jesus takes these bits of creation, which represent the whole, and invites all to participate in an act of sharing which is also an act of sacrifice. The prayer of consecration in the Eucharist, shaped through the work of the Early Church

Fathers, is an exact replication of the story and the process of the creed. To give self into the abyss of confrontation with the wisdom and sophistication of the world's religious and political systems, facing the Passover and exile into darkness, and totally dependent upon the call and care of God to bring light and warmth that will open out a new possibility of life. As Jesus, in the prayer of consecration is called, crucified and raised, so this is the journey of the bread and the wine (the everydayness of creation) and of each participant willing to follow in this way of sacrifice and sharing.

In this way, each person at this particular party becomes a sacrament – a sign to others present and beyond. Thus, each is called into a personal journey, which also becomes a way of witness: discipleship involves both elements. The task of discernment is to recognise the particular part each is called to be, in order to assist personal formation and appropriate public witness.

The nature of such a double call – to a personal and public identity and role – means that participation in the party gives a particular kind of fragrance – a sense and style that cannot be put into words or systems, but rather emerges as a confidence towards a certain direction, a commitment to inclusivity and a determination to notice those who are normally ignored and overlooked. This is the fragrance of the Trinity, something that can be tasted but not easily appropriated.

This means that as people leave the Party of the Eucharist, they are not going 'home', into a comfortable private space, but rather they have become caught up in the triumphal procession of Christ, guiding each disciple towards the place of witness. Often this will be a journey replicating the creedal path, and beginning by seeking the lowest way.

For Jesus and his followers, this path led to Kidron – a place for further prayer and testing, before being overwhelmed by the challenges of human wisdoms and systems devised solely according to the canons of human experience and assessment.

The party equips disciples for the creedal journey, for life in the Trinity, by drawing each attendee deeply into the mysteries of the journey, and into thanksgiving for the life-giving power and promise of the process – but through the risk of sacrifice and sharing, stepping outside of the securities of human understanding into a very different kind of flow in the forces of creation.

And because the weeds continue to grow, the process of this party, this Eucharistic gathering, needs to continue as a reference point and reminder to disciples of the Way, the Truth and the Life. Living in the Trinity is to enter into this drama whereby creation and creatures are tested, refined, and called to step beyond the structures of human wisdom and manageable experience, into the darkness which entombs and opens up new possibilities.

This party introduces us to what the Fathers called the second mystery. The first mystery was the mystery of creation, with all its joys and challenges. The second mystery is the mystery of salvation – the particular gift of Christ. Creation needs salvation. The reality of fallenness requires resurrection. Human experience provides an agenda to wrestle with the mystery of creation, often handled through being led by our lustfulness for our own immediate wellbeing. A larger version of such lustfulness can be concern for the wellbeing of the planet – while being blind to the faithful processes of salvation to which the whole of creation is subject.

Within this context of the two mysteries, the Fathers saw the task of the church as being to enable three movements: the number is significant as being within the frame of the Trinity. The framework was that of the church building – a primary venue for enabling the party plan.

The nave is the body of the church, where worshippers bring their bodies, their createdness. This is to take the lowest place. The service of Eucharist calls us towards the sanctuary, where the angels sing 'Holy, Holy, Holy' – the song of the Trinity. The sanctuary is where the soul, the capacity within the body to look beyond createdness, can be ministered to – through moving the focus from the experience of embodiment as a predominant reference point, in order to become open to our Maker and Redeemer: the two mysteries of creation now enveloped by salvation.

The liturgy accepts our embodiedness and then, after confession, nourishment from scripture and focussing in prayer, the soul is prepared to be called into a different environment and atmosphere – that of *salvus* or true health. The rhythm of joining with others and with the angels to sing the song of the Trinity, Holy, Holy, Holy.

But the journey does not end here, because the final point for human being is the altar – where body and soul offer their fragilities, their incompleteness, and their need for healing, hope and heaven. The altar is the place where offering in made and blessing received. Giving the brokenness of body and soul to be made whole in a deeper way. This Holy Spirit indwells the worshipper who then proceeds back through the sanctuary and the nave, into the teeming creation apparently dominated by seeming efforts of trying to order life with little sense or search for the second mystery of salvation.

For the Fathers, these three movements – the body in the nave, the soul in the sanctuary, the spirit of healing and wholeness at the altar, provides the shaping for living in the Trinity. For accepting the true calling of the soil, the seed and the sunshine: the Creator, creation with its potential, and salvation infusing all with glory. There is a profound sense in which participation in such a Eucharistic party leaves people with a testing kind of hangover!

7

Praying in the Trinity

How does living in the Trinity, being in the image of the Trinity, effect our approach to prayer? When St. Augustine explores the Trinity through the imagery of the Lover, the Beloved and the Love between them, there is a dynamism of active connection and mutual desire for wellbeing. Love given, received and expressed. For human beings the call to live in love given, received and expressed in ways which enable this dynamic of mutuality and oneness.

Yet Augustine points out that such love is never a closed circle of self-reference. Marriage would be an illustration of love given, received and expressed in ways that flow into wider relationships and the making of community. Thus the measure of marriage, as of any relationship between different parties, is not just the flourishing of those directly concerned, but also includes the benefits and blessings given into the wider community. Any relationship, in which two discover a third connecting element that strengthens their oneness, becomes a sacrament to nourish and encourage all who are privileged to be touched by it. Love is always an invitation that invites difference into oneness of grace and goodness. Love given, received and expressed always overflows towards those in need of being embraced by such salvation. This is why the household is so important in scripture: a place not of a limited 'family' circle of love, but a frame for including all kinds of other people in a single dynamic of care and support.

Jesus goes in and out of households because they are open to public engagement, and not closed in on themselves. Such acting out of the challenging dynamic of love is much more difficult in a time of security locks and barred windows. The sharing of love becomes restricted and undermined by a predominance of process and control.

Paul highlights the model for koinonia, the way Christians are called to make communities and households, in the final words of his second letter to the Corinthians: "the grace of our Lord Jesus Christ, the love of God and the community of the Holy Spirit".

To pray as people living in the Trinity, and owning that we are made in the image of the Trinity, is to own this calling to be inhabitants of such households and communities. Prayer can never be a private engagement with God, some kind of direct line seeking guidance for the self. Rather, in the words of the Orthodox theological Kallistos Ware, in prayer "we find ourselves caught up in a conversation that is already in progress, the eternal dialogue of the Trinity".[1]

---

[1] Sobernost 8:2 (1986).

This is the true context and purpose of prayer – not a private conversation, nor the privileged engagement of a group gathered in church for worship, but always participation in the whole conversation of the mysterion: creation receiving salvation in the life of the Trinity. Too often disciples settle for something much more circumscribed, and therefore are susceptible to becoming limited by the contours of what can be our own 'experience'. Leading intercessions in church, or schemes for private devotion, can easily succumb to such a temptation.

Whereas prayer properly understood is to bring the giving and receiving of love through which human being unfolds, into the light and warmth of the Holy Spirit – the power and purposes of God being drawn out of creation for its proper fulfilment. This 'conversation' is already in progress, the flow into creation of goodness and grace. Such prayer does not stop when we are not self-consciously participating, and when we do try to open ourselves it is into a flow that embraces so much more than ourselves or our own context.

Therefore households and communities are the proper sites of prayer, always open to further embrace into greater possibilities and webs of relations. Prayer should not be so much a focus on 'what do I need to say to the Lord, and what has he got to say to me?' – but rather 'what have I been missing by closing my doors and getting on with life while ignoring this conversation and all its amazing implications?'

Prayer is to become open to the warmth and light of love as the dynamic which joins every Lover and Beloved in an ever greater sense of koinonia. Participation depends less upon creating a mood of quiet receptivity – which again subtly places the focus on the person or group preparing – but rather a desire to open eyes wider, notice the unnoticed, and be drawn into the creedal process which will always seek to begin anew in the lowest place. This conversation is always in process, and prayer is the attempt to plug in more self-consciously, so that actions and attitudes can be better informed by warmth and light as good news for others. There is an essential Catholicity about the nature of Christian prayer.

The life of the Trinity unfolds through persons. The Latin word 'persona' brings together two words: sonare, from which we get sonorous – sound: and per, which means through. A person, a persona means sounding through. The music, the conversation of God sounds through persons, within the Trinity, and in human beings made in the image of the Trinity. To be a person is to be able to receive and give the warmth and life of God as love. This power flows through creatures whether we notice it or not. It is the source of goodness, beauty, conscience, sacrificial service of others. But it is most fully appreciated and magnified through a prayerfulness which tries to pay particular attention to the sounding and to thereby make the self more open to being the conduit through which lifegiving love can feely pass.

Such love is a form of power which can be blessed and directed through prayerful attention and co-operation. It emphasises the breadth and inclusivity of the conversation which can pass through human creatures. In Genesis 1[26] the creation includes the framing "let us make humankind

in our own image". The image is plural – the dynamics of
the Trinity and the dynamics sounding through each person
made in this way. Thus, when we pray for the victims of
terrorism or forced migration, the prayer is not simply for
God to do something for them: to make these poor people
safer and happier. This form of intercession can be a means
of shifting a pressure from our consciences into God's hands,
to help our own 'experience' of helplessness be mitigated.
Even to give us permission to get on with our lives and leave
the matter to God.

Rather we are praying into a conversation which we cannot
step away from, and in which ourselves, our brothers and
sisters who are suffering, and all the systems and failings of
the world are caught up. To be a person is to become more
self-conscious as being someone through whom the spirit of
warmth and light can flow, despite the darkness and death so
evident to mere human experience. This connectivity will
inform our actions and attitudes in relation to the suffering,
in relation to systems that are failing, and in relation to the
wider dynamic between dark and light, depression and hope.

Thus, prayer closes the apparent gap between the self
and wider concerns, and empowers those who pray to
live and act and intercede as part of the situation in all its
complexity and difficulty. Such an approach to praying no
longer 'masters' or secures the agendas we face – the seeking
of stability and success that so easily becomes the subject
of both private and public prayer. Rather it draws each of
us more fully into being a part of the process of the life of
the Trinity. A single offering of salvation that is mediated

through households and communities by ever breaking them open to receive new elements and opportunities.

This may mean similar practical outcomes to those who might be associated with a more classical approach asking God to better order things – for instance work on immigration controls, relief efforts or peace building. But the crucial difference engendered by praying that aims at entry into a continuing conversation is that the divisions of culture and context are now transcended by owning an inevitable involvement in the call of others – especially those who seem distant and beyond the reach of the more immediate levels of human resourcing through which we tend to live.

Prayer as part of this Trinitarian conversation is a matter of the heart, which will inform but also transcend the skills of the 'head': love knows no boundaries in terms of reaching out to need through the commitment of self-sacrifice. Generosity and grace fuel an energy to go more than the extra mile, and to seek ways of the self being part of the agency of salvation. There is one God, one conversation, one direction, unfolding through the dynamic of the Trinity.

Such an approach does not simplify our sense of direction; rather it introduces extra layers of complexity, and therefore requires more paying attention to the sound of love sent to pass through us. Prayer becomes more important rather than merely part of a process of reflection and response.

An important biblical image which explores this dynamic of prayer is that of marriage. In Genesis we learn that the creation of humankind is expressed by the profound mystery "male and female he created them" Genesis 1(27). Jesus reinforces this foundational mystery by confirming that "the two shall become one". Male and female joined in love to become witnesses and agents of love for others too. Marriage is a public institution as well as a private commitment – this is the point of the first sign of the Gospel in St John Chapter 2. Love sounds through each partner is a way which joins different elements into a witness for salvation through the households and communities which enable human life to unfold securely.

This picture of marriage provokes an interesting challenge to more modern concerns about equality. Within such a frame even marriage has become an assessable, negotiable contract, rather than the gift of a divine mystery. Of course, there will always be failures and divorces due to human imperfection, alongside the huge spectrum of gender and relationship possibilities evident between those of a man and a woman in holy wedlock and a man and a woman in a single state.

Yet such diversity needs a frame for ordering, and as prayer seeks to be open to the sounding through of love at every point on such a spectrum, the primary marker of marriage between a man and woman as a rich kernel to household or community needs to be noticed.

The breadth and complexity of the divine conversation which prayer is privileged to enter, nonetheless has markers in the Gospel of the Christ that are important shapers of how to evaluate our instincts and be called into the costly disciplines of giving the self into an apparent darkness that might invite the sacrifice of immediate experience and aspiration for a deeper flow. Given the power of human lustfulness, issues of sexuality and identity need to be prayed into this broad Trinitarian conversation – not only to extend possibilities by noticing and affirming the previously unnoticed, but also to take seriously markers which might lay down challenges to an easy privileging of what we feel or experience.

Love needs space for greater inclusivity, but love also requires faithfulness to the signs whereby greater grace might be modelled so as to provide markers within the way of expanding salvation to all of creation. In this way the love that is the life of the Trinity helps place the particular in the larger picture of salvation, and enables practical contributions to be shaped and offered as 'part' of the process, along with many other elements raised up for specific purposes within the overall project.

Acts Chapters 2 and 4 give glimpses of how such a diversity of contributions emerging from the conversation in prayer can be knitted together for the common flourishing of all, and for the particular care of those in need. The conversation is anything but ethereal: it is always part of incarnation, the practical manifestation of love in the midst of the human search for glory and eternity. The mystical always needs to issue in the material. In fact, in the Eucharist the mystical issues through the material, both in the liturgy and in the sending out of the participants to engage further in the calls of the conversation.

Such prayer provides a vision to enable greater participation in transforming the unfolding of history. An example would be a church praying in a way that included the bringing of food to be distributed to the hungry. A simple transaction of conversation into political and social outcomes on the side of grace and targeting those normally unnoticed. Markers of history being reshaped as acting out of the conversation that is the life of the Trinity, bringing signs of salvation into the groaning of creation. Love made flesh to engender faith, hope and more love. Too easily we can observe such work as 'social action', and only a part of the Gospel – rather than recognising it as a clear outflowing of the salvation the Gospel is given to enable.

Such praying needs to inform how we live in marriages, households and in communities, and to be the test and interpreter of more 'mystical' experiences in prayer.

8

Trinity and Theology

Theology involves thinking through issues in words about God – the Word. It bears witness to the reality that in God life is about a process of communication and expression: the life of the Trinity in creation and in salvation.

To think is to disturb the moment and begin to identify new possibilities. Thinking is the ability to fracture the status quo in order to be able to perceive new things. A mundane example would be thinking that produces a shopping list – opening up possibilities about food, travel, health and even happiness. Light keeps trying to enter the dullness of standing still or not considering further possibilities.

Education and maturity are established ways of trying to understand how best to develop and to school this inner energy which emerges as thinking, particularly because its usefulness and creativity can often unfold into chaos and destructiveness. Spirituality might be described as thinking schooled by paying close attention to Jesus Christ, the purposes of the Father and the power of the Spirit.

By its very nature thinking produces disturbance and unsettlement. And this will be as true of theology as of any other discipline. Theology therefore cannot be reduced to formulas for belief or behaviour. The ever approaching light and warmth of the Spirit continues to disturb and invite into newness – often by the way of the cross. This is what makes theology, or Christian thinking, so distinctive – and very different from scientific reason which seeks to build confidently and accumulatively through analysis of human experience and a trust in systems to control and shape.

At the heart of Christian theology lies fraction – the process of the Eucharist, the way of the Trinity. Such wisdom is often recognised by poetry, exposing the limitations of words and ideas through the exploration of insights not yet grasped, but possibly hidden in what has been presented. By breaking open the words, the fresh thinking of the imagination can be set free – though often through hints rather than the tangible outcomes required by science. Christian theology will always rest in a poetic spirituality which privileges not-knowing over what is known, and begins by admitting the imperfection and failings of even the best of human endeavours. The prism of the cross remains central – the sign of poetic fracture.

Jesus is the manifestation in human being of this unsettling, costly creativity whereby salvation can redeem creation. In Him disciples 'do' theology – that is the prayerful thinking that emerges in costly action for the sake of the always mysterious unfolding of divine life. This was the message of Paul's sermon to the philosophers at the Areopagus – we are called to begin by recognising that we worship an unknown God – revealed through the mystery of death and resurrection, rather than through human reason and systems. The key is 'The resurrection of the dead'. His hearers were unsettled. Some scoffed and some said that they would think and then hear Paul further. One of those who heard and responded was Dionysius the Areopogite.

In the fifth century a Christian thinker influenced by Neo-Platonism styled himself Dionysius the Areopogite. This gave credibility to his thinking by claiming such a direct association with St Paul. He held, with Plato, that the human soul is on a journey towards deification – being made more fully part of God, of the Absolute; the One. The second letter of Peter echoes a similar theme in claiming that through the Christian life "you may escape from the corruption that is in the world because of passion" – i.e. human lustfulness draws our focus too closely around ourselves and we become closed to participating in the greater fullness of God. The Christian is called "to become partakers of the divine nature", to recognise that we are living in the Trinity.

To do this Dionysius discerned three ways of thinking for the Christian – each a way of unsettlement. First the way of what he termed 'affirmative theology'. Thinking about what we can see and experience, and thanking God for being with us in our fleshliness. We can experience God's presence and power: seeds knowing warmth and light.

Second, he identifies 'negative theology'. The recognition that despite knowing something of God's presence and power, we see but through a glass darkly, because He is so much greater, and each of us is only a tiny bit in a huge universe. Thus, while affirmative theology emerges in the prayer of discernment and exploration of the conversation, negative theology reduces the thinker to a stunned silence – just like being plunged into the darkness of the soil, and losing contact with every familiar marker and comfort. The instinct to seek warmth and light seems to be totally submerged into helplessness and an overwhelming complexity.

Third, Dionysius talks about 'speculative theology', which takes our thinking beyond affirming what we know, and beyond accepting the negativity of our tiny helplessness – into a place where the interplay between knowing and not knowing opens us to a deeper register of the Spirit, which we experience as 'union with God'. Illumination and purgation, in the traditional terms, both disturb and destabilise in a way that the very helplessness of confusion can become a spiritual state within which darkness and frustration can be miraculously touched with a sense of the presence of God – not to crystallise the illuminations of affirmation, nor to disperse the confusions of negation, but simply to give a sense of assurance that the light and warmth of love remain active and in richer prospect.

To explore this insight Dionysius introduces the word 'hierarchy'. Arché means the principle of ordering. Hieros is of God. We tend to see hierarchy as a pyramid of ordered roles, from the boss to the most junior person. Hierarchy in this sense is not popular in a world seeking rights and democracy as a means of equal individual participation. But for Dionysius, hierarchy is simply the proper ordering that

God designs so that each element can flourish appropriately. It is a way of ordering difference creatively, not of distributing power unevenly to reinforce systems of the control of some by others. St Paul's image of the Body and Jesus' image of the kingdom are similar pictures of a divine ordering for all of the parts, each in their proper place.   In this space hierarchy is essential and life-giving.

Dionysius pointed towards a celestial hierarchy. Reading from Scripture, he discerned nine orders of angels, in three cohorts. The first order is Seraphim, Cherubim and Thrones. The second order is Dominions, Virtues and Powers. The third is Principalities, Archangels and Angels.

A later medieval writer noticed that in Psalm 33 verse 2 God is to be praised on the ten string lute. The author suggested that this would be the nine orders of angels, plus humankind. Thus, humanity needed to be in harmony with the angels and the celestial hierarchy if God is to be properly praised. Humanity living in the Trinity, fully embraced in the greater glory of creation as represented by the angelic orders.

Further, Dionysius posited an ecclesiastical hierarchy. Again nine ranks in three orders. In the first rank are the three sacraments, which he identified as Baptism Eucharist and Extreme Unction (being anointed for death). The tools God has given to enable the journey of what we are calling the life of the Trinity – from heights to depths to being raised up: the creedal sequence.

The second rank in the ecclesiastical hierarchy is what he calls 'the teaching church: Bishops, Priests and Deacons'.

Those called by God to safeguard and minister the gifts God provides for his people – scripture, sacraments and creeds. The resources to anchor thinking within the tradition: what will be is consonant with what has already been given.

The third rank is 'the learning church: Monks (the committed disciples in our terms), Catechumens (i.e. those who need to be taught more about the faith), and finally 'the burial of the dead' (the reality of the human journey into the creedal process).

What is interesting for our purposes is that these orders do not signify a ranking according to importance, but each has a part to play in the salvation of creation. Our task is not to capture or over-explain these callings, but to discern our particular calling in inhabiting the contribution we have been made to fulfil. Each of us needs to be able to think and pray in a way that disturbs any obvious assumptions, and opens us to a challenging call and commitment.

Further, such discernment should provide a frame within which we are content to operate, so that further disturbance is about the fulfilling of this calling, not an unrealistic attempt to escape into a different order. There is an underlying discipline and focus.

And within this hierarchy or divine ordering, each of us has two tasks. First, to learn from the rank above, as agents of particularly appropriate love and support especially to those below. In this way God's grace is particularly focussed upon relationships which will allow and enable appropriate connection within the Body of Christ and the ordering of creation for salvation.

Without being distracted by the particular categories Dionysius chooses to identify, it is an important challenge to explore what divine ordering should look like for the church and for her disciples to be faithful to the unfolding of the life in the Trinity, in a way that tries to allow the most radical freedom of possibilities for new life to be shaped in order to allow real impact in everyday lives by taking seriously the relationships that God has already crafted and sanctified.

In this sense Dionysius challenges each person to explore their own vocation with particular reference to the vocations of other people and structures that have been placed around them – and from such discernment, often enriched by the way of the cross, to be better empowered in witness, and in contributing to the grace of glory.

Spiritual discernment, even via the way of Calvary, needs to issue in disciplined outcomes – within a divine order. Ephesians chapter 4 makes this clear with its enumeration of different but essentially complementary ministries for the building up of the Body.

Moreover we need to discern the place of learning, of sacraments, of the burial of the dead in our spiritual ecologies. How best is vocation ordered according to God's principles, so that life in the Trinity may flow to greatest effect. Together such 'perfecting of each singularly and all together' will manifest more fully what Dionysius terms 'the Community of Love'. This is a process which unfolds through the disturbance that can clarify vocation by looking more closely at the places from where we might receive, and towards those to whom we shall especially concentrate our giving. Disturbance is for a purpose not of our own choosing, but to better enable our recognition of God's plan and our call to be of service within it – both through being nourished, and through the giving of ourselves.

In this Dionysius teaches the disciple that the ability to think is the ability to discern vocation through continuing disturbance – but always within the frame of God's purposes. Vocation ceases to be a personal matter, and instead becomes more focussed participation within the Body of Christ. The spiritual journey is about seeking our appropriate place within the divine ordering – not for personal perfecting, but for a challenging interchange with other elements of the unfolding life of the Trinity – so that the creedal dynamic of heights, depths and new life can be best channelled.

We "live and move and have our being" in God (Acts 17) but Paul was clear that this miracle unfolds through 'the good news of the Resurrection of the dead'. Only life in the Trinity can enable such a miracle.

Sin remains the temptation to miss the mark towards which we are called, by putting our own agenda and stability before the challenging unevenness of finding the place from which we can best contribute to the divine ordering of salvation. Dionysius was clear about this temptation, and his schemes of hierarchy provide an invitation to take seriously the principles, while claiming a proper freedom to describe this necessary ranking in our own terms.

The direction and the outcomes are what he would have recognised as deification: the ordering of life in the Trinity. He offers an attractive image: "if we can find our place in the order and own it... it will be like the soul dancing with God in the life of the Trinity".

9

Trinity and Society

Psalm 62 recognises the power that belongs to God, and the love that belongs to God. Society can be seen as the frame we create to try to reconcile love and power.

In the liturgy the creed serves as the public statement of a public process that is designed to embrace everybody in the flow of creation receiving salvation. The journey is from heights to depths to new heights through the corporation of the church, the communion of saints, the forgiveness of sins, the resurrection of the body and the life everlasting.

The process is unending and works by the continuing destabilising of established positions, calling for renewed faith in the mysterious engagement with the power of darkness. While much of human history is a testament to building islands of resistance to this flow of divine life, through minimising the powers of sin/selfishness, and overestimating the human capacity to take over direction of stresses and fractures which keep appearing, the Christian Gospel ever calls for risking the invitation that in God's power a different kind of security and stability can be discovered. A divine ordering which works with unevenness and complexity, and which, against the odds, aims to involve every child of God who can be encouraged to respond. Thus society is to be constituted not simply through human assessments, ideas and schemes, but always as refined and re-formed through this often painful process. Human history witnesses to the inevitability of disruption, and yet human endeavour so often stops at trying to control and preserve.

Both Jesus and Paul accepted the shaping of society by the Roman system. Jesus paid taxes to enable the public provision of security and services, and Paul not only claimed the privileges of citizenship, but initiated for the growing church the Roman model of devolution that kept a central authority and local expressions in a tension that recognised the importance of honouring both elements.

Living in the Trinity highlights some important realities for the ordering and sustaining of society. One is the reality of interdependence: each part counts, even those which in Pauline language, might appear to be 'unseemly'. There is a deep interconnectivity between what might otherwise be experienced as separated parts. The Green Movement is helping contemporary people to recognise a common citizenship as inhabitants of the earth. In the Trinity such interdependence is far more radical and far-reaching – into eternity.

The lesson is that the fruit which we bear is for the benefit of others. There needs to be ownership of a radical mutuality, which must include friendship with strangers and sympathetic engagement with enemies – two of the most revolutionary and provocative teachings of Jesus. Citizenship needs to be bigger than membership, even if society needs to be shaped through more local centres of service and identity. Seeds need particular contexts within to flourish, but always as part of a wider ecology where different contributions create life, and sometimes obstacles. In this sense attempts to form society will always mirror nature.

The overarching reality is the flow of creation. Yet people need pools of meaning and identity: a sense of place and locality. Jesus points to the handling of this potential tension between local and universal by stressing the role of intimacy. The strange word he chooses to talk about his Father is Abba – which really means 'Daddy': the language of a small child totally dependent upon a very local context and set of restricted relationships.

Abba indicates both the need for a real intimacy or closeness, and yet the articulation of a huge reality, as yet unknown, but safely vested in the parent who provides the bridge between cot and community in its widest possibilities. The child has a small inclination of a reality which is represented to it in a way that will allow controlled access and engagement. Jesus invites each child to trust in this intimacy as the key to being able to recognise and inhabit a far greater interdependence. This recognition and acceptance will play out through the particularities of vocation, as described by Dionysius, and through ever seeking to envision the amazing scale of the greater interdependence which is creation. Each child needs to grow up with being able to know, and to trust in the possibilities which will only ever be intimations of a much greater unknown.

This dynamic is unfolded through a number of foundational scenarios. The Good Samaritan provides a response to the lawyer's desire for a definition to capture 'neighbourliness'. The story makes the self the key to any definition – love your neighbour as yourself, and when the point is established, be committed to 'go and do likewise'. The aim is to practice intimacy as love in a real context, with all its limitations, but then to trust this defining experience into the unknown.

Further, in the spirit of Dionysius, the Good Samaritan looks down to the level below himself: he is comfortable and busy, on the floor is a bruised and beaten person needing 'ministry' through intimacy. He raises this person towards his own 'level' – a safe place, money and people to provide for his needs. But – he goes further, in that he tells the carer, the innkeeper, to maintain this system – because they can both look upwards to a rank of teaching that grace can provide. The 'salvation' operates through an intimacy that reaches out below, and a trust in the power of grace which extends from above.

In terms of society, intimacy creates connection, systems of care and the potential for their extension. The base of what can be known is ever expanding, but always within a framework of trust in a greater interdependence and intimacy: an 'unknown' intuition that can come from above in Dionysian terms, to connect with the needs below. The partnership between these two sources and expressions of intimacy creates the structures and vision for society. Each of the three characters in the story of the Good Samaritan will no doubt continue to live their own lives, but interdependent in a society created by compassion, careful organisation and confident commitment. A 'victim' of the breakdown of society has been restored in a way that is also restorative of society itself.

Another important picture is that of the triumphal entry of Jesus into Jerusalem. Gathered in this 'society' were Jesus' followers, who had been carefully schooled in the art of intimacy for the kingdom; those who followed because they had witnessed the blessings that intimacy could bring; and those going to the Temple for the more formalised ordering of intimacy through systems of ritual and sacrifice. A thriving, joyful 'society' on the move, following the Son of the Father, joined in a common spirit of faith and hope and love. But then love meets power. This free flowing intimacy seems dangerous and full of unknown possibilities. The instinct of the 'authorities' is to protect what knowledge has securely established by way of political and religious systems. The 'crowd' soon get the point. The free flow of intimacy soon gives way to the chant "we have no king but Caesar". The Son of the Father, the prompter of the Spirit, is subject to a different chant "crucify him".

The flow of the life of the Trinity to embrace the interdependence of these different elements and perspectives meets the islands of resistance and darkness ensues. Darkness was over the whole land. Power is accumulated and exercised for control, and not for inclusion; for law through boundaries rather than love connecting differences.

Throughout history, in the spirit of the Good Samaritan, Christians have set up systems of intimacy, to allow love to connect those below with the grace above. Examples would be William Wilberforce and attempts to abolish slavery. But the weeds of insecurity and the desire for the boundaries which promise security through exclusion keep arising. The darkness of this collision of power for survival meeting intimacy for inclusion can often seem to prevail and hang over the land.

This is why the story of life in the Trinity in the creedal declaration is such an important safeguard for public welfare and the shaping of society in a way that invites love to order power, rather than the opposite transaction.

For Christians to be creative citizens in the ways envisaged by Jesus and by St Paul – we need to cultivate the courage of the Good Samaritan whereby we keep trying to set up systems to care for and unite people in that goodness which comes from above (the power of love). This must be a faithful strategy amidst the realities of the temptation for established systems of human organisation to only trust in the love of power. The key is the willingness to go the extra mile in terms of cost to self – the sacrifice that turns intimacy into systems of love.

Society needs systems; the question is about their source and their goal. Such systems need to be created in response to the indicators of genuine human need, struggle and violent dysfunction. The darkness will always be a feature, to enable their robustness to be brought down and yet rise again as a manifestation of the creedal process which is not just the story of the Saviour, but also the necessary story of every society.

In the story of the Centurion who came to Jesus seeking healing for his servant in Luke chapter 7, we are given another clue for the ordering of society. The Centurion feels that he is not worthy for Jesus to come to his house – he appeals to the exercise of 'authority'. Jesus comments "never have I seen such faith, not even in Israel" (i.e. among God's called and chosen people). The Roman Centurion had such faith because he was within a system of Empire that embraced everybody in an ordering that allowed local intimacies and cultures, but always with some kind of allegiance to a much greater and more inclusive reality. 'Just give a word'. This notion of a common law is still the backbone of many attempts to create society. There can be an approach to law that gives space for love to bring healing, hope and richer connections between different cultures and experiences.

Jesus says "never have I seen such faith" – that is a system whereby a society might function to enable the intimacy which brings healing and hope, especially to those 'below' the line of normal expectations.

The Trinity flowing through society brings divine life right into our midst, but there will always be disruption and darkness. But contributions need to be made from victims, from operators of systems and from those inspired to create them.

10

Trinity and Worship

Holy, holy, holy! Lord God Almighty!
Early in the morning our song shall rise to Thee;
Holy, holy, holy, merciful and mighty!
God in three Persons blessed Trinity!

Holy, holy, holy! All the saints adore Thee,
Casting down their golden crowns around the glassy sea;
Cherubim and seraphim falling down before Thee,
Who was, and is, and evermore shall be.

Holy, holy, holy! Though the darkness hide Thee,
Though the eye of sinful man Thy glory may not see;
Only Thou art holy; there is none beside Thee,
Perfect in pow'r, in love, and purity.

Holy, holy, holy! Lord God Almighty!
All Thy works shall praise Thy Name, in earth, and sky,
and sea;

Holy, holy, holy; merciful and mighty!
God in three Persons, blessed Trinity!

Reginald Heber, 1826

Much worship can be seen to presuppose a binary state of reality. A contrast between the material and mystical or more purely spiritual realm. The assumption can be that the mystical is holy and takes us closer to God, his real power and purposes, while the material is more limited, transient and partial.

The implication is that worship provides an opportunity for reflection which shapes and directs the 'inner' life, to better enable the disciple to then go into the 'world' to try to put the insights and inspiration received into practice. People are encouraged to come to church for supervised prayers, that will provide an appropriate frame and direction for the rest of their lives.

This approach might seem to be reinforced by St Paul's great image in Roman's chapter 8 of the whole creation groaning in labour pains to enable the light and warmth of the Creator to flow more effectively. However, as St Paul recognised with his understanding of resurrection, it is the labour pains which create the new life: the very struggle of the Trinity is at work, bringing new life to birth.

Thus prayer for an individual or a church group can never be understood simply as a period of reflection apart from the pressures of everyday life. Rather, prayer should be part of the experience of labour pains – a struggling engagement with the potential for the birthing of new life – reflection always in the midst of action and its stresses.

Labour pains provide a model not just of no escape from the realities of the process, but more, needing to accept an uncertainty about both timescales and the likely outcomes. There can be no handing over of aspiration to God – only a struggling participation in the as yet new life He is bringing to birth in and through our bodies. The contemporary emphasis upon controlling both the timing of birth and the process of labour undermines the more natural realities of facing the unknown in terms of unfolding experience and with regard to likely outcomes.

The development of methods and manuals for prayer and the sophistication of liturgical resources and frameworks can tend to minimise this challenging confrontation with the life of the Trinity calling out birth in ways and forms which will be beyond our immediate control. In worship there is a vital distinction between co-operation and control. This means that worship can never focus around us wanting to feel better about ourselves or our place in the world. These proper concerns will always have to be recognised as part of the material through which the life of the Trinity can be expressed – always for the sake of the greater whole. This is the real work of the Holy Spirit.

Moreover the genuine unknowingness of outcomes needs to inform both the atmosphere and the attitude given prominence in worship. This is especially important given that public worship should be, in one sense, like a mass labour ward! The challenge is to join together the new lives being born through individuals and smaller groups into the appropriate birth and refining of the systems necessary to providing framing, security and the blessings of community.

This means that to pray or to attend worship in church will always be a risky process, stepping into a dynamic that brings into sharp and stressful focus what is happening in human lives, and what could be brought to birth. And, of course, this challenging call is always within the framework of the creedal journey which places the descent into darkness as a key element in the process which can produce new life.

This context is clearly very different from a routine of attending a service, sitting and standing as instructed, and joining in pre-prepared statements of concern and aspiration. At the heart of worship there needs to be the journey of Jesus – from life to death to new life – as the way for others to follow. To worship should involve taking a risk by stepping into the unknown, where ones very self is to be subject to new call and challenge.

The occasion should provide opportunity to look below and above, in the way of Dionysius and of the Good Samaritan. Paul points towards this approach in the first chapter of Romans, by giving a focus towards Jesus, born of David, into the fleshliness 'below', yet being declared the Son of God by the power of the Spirit of holiness, the guidance and the grace from above. From the conjunction of flesh and spirit, of lower and higher levels, flows grace as action and witness in the calling of the everyday world towards glory and eternity.

This is why confession is so central, because it requires ownership of falling and frailty, and thus our unfitness to bring to birth any goodness without the indwelling and guidance of a purifying and purposeful Holy Spirit. The miracle of new life can only emerge with God's guidance and help – on our own we will lack the resources and the capacity.

In this sense confession becomes the moment of unsettlement. Thus worship should be a seeking not of stability and security, but a willingness to be called into the unsettling effects of thinking anew about our work and witness so that we are better prepared to step into new spaces ready to participate in the labour pains through which the indwelling of the Trinity unfolds. Public worship needs to issue in a renewed sense of public direction and service.

Each worshipper brings their body into the nave, to be drawn, with others, into the sanctuary, and blessed by the Spirit of holiness, and then together to offer the sacrifice of self at the altar on which brokenness can be laid - in the sure and certain faith of the resurrection of healing and hope.

These insights about worship and the invitation to pray in the Trinity were given expression in the work of Reginald Heber, who lived in the late eighteenth and early nineteenth century. For sixteen years he was a county parson in Hodnot in Shropshire, the home of his family. He had studied in Oxford, and discovered gifts as a poet. This is an important element for worship. Prose too easily becomes closed into set meanings and messages: poetry preserves the capacity for enabling the 'thinking' that breaks open words and phrases to ever see new things – none of which become definitive, but always indicative of what the Spirit might be saying.

When Heber was exploring his own vocational journey, he wrote to a friend "pray for me that I may have my eyes open to the truth". Prayer is an active state of being open to the unfolding of truth, not a mere recitation of apparently established and static statements. Prayer is being open to new life, not being soaked in closed systems. An example of public worship in his parish was the emergence of a willingness to support the Society for the Propagation of the Gospel – that is to be joined in the birth pangs of others within the wider Christian fellowship through sacrificial giving.

He was invited to become Bishop of Calcutta, and despite some hesitation because of his wife Amelia and their young daughter, he decided to accept and was consecrated in Lambeth Palace Chapel in London on 1st June 1823. They arrived in India in October 1823. His calling was into radically unpredictable birth pangs, for himself and his family, and for the emerging Anglican Church in India. The Diocese of Calcutta had been established in 1814. Heber had a very short ministry in India – he died in April 1826. In his time he reached out to people trapped in the human hierarchy of the caste system, and tried to connect them with higher aspirations for grace to be shared together. He met with Hindu leaders too: looking 'below' and 'above' to try and offer ways of more wholesome connection, ever within what was clearly a very rigid system of control. Birth pangs do not always deliver bonny new life in pristine condition. Often birth pangs are struggles within which much of life has to be lived – in stress and the offering of partial contributions.

Heber became an accomplished hymn writer – and one of his most famous works is 'Holy, Holy, Holy' - worship in the Trinity. He lived in a time when the power and beauty of music in public worship was being discovered – through the work of people such as Charles Wesley. Singing together lifts people out of a sense of individual struggle into a taste of a wider glory through which the flow of God's presence and power can be known. However, when he published a book of hymns in 1819, the Archbishop of Canterbury was not willing to contribute a preface – such was official nervousness about the unknown forces which music in public worship might release.

Heber knew that hymns created an atmosphere which helped to draw people's souls from the nave towards the sanctuary, better prepared to give the self into sacrificial service at the altar, for the wellbeing of the whole of society.

The hymn Holy, Holy, Holy draws human hearts into the life of the Trinity. It develops a theme which is central to the Book of Revelation: the Trinity is God almighty, all embracing, and the centre of the worship of all creatures. Thus the hymn begins by enabling worshippers to pray themselves more consciously into the Trinity through this ancient invocation. "Early in the morning, our song shall rise to thee." Life begins by birth into a new day, with songs rising to the heights of God's call to glory. To sing is to participate in trying to articulate and share this calling. To recognise that the first instinct of human being is to look upwards (Dionysius) and to seek to be raised.

Moreover the One to be met in the heights to which we are made to aspire is 'merciful and mighty' – that is, love and power in perfect harmony. Too often human aspiration leads to missing the mark and lowering our sights towards ourselves because in the search love and power become separate, and in conflict. This would be the picture framing the trial, torture and execution of Jesus.

This fallen dynamic has been inhabited by the Son, so that to be reminded of 'God in three persons' is to remember that the involvement of the Trinity is to bring blessings towards every element of what appears to be a hopelessly divided ecology created by human centred endeavours. The key to salvation, true health, is to enter into this set of relationships – persons showing faith in the possibilities of a more perfect harmony.

Because of this living set of relations which can embrace the whole range of human experience, from aspiration to descent into darkness to the welcome of warmth and light calling out new growth, so "all the saints adore thee". This is the life and journey of all who accept the invitation into discipleship - all who have gone before, every contemporary so commissioned, and every person yet to come: the whole of creation is embraced and invited to join in this song of 'Holy, Holy, and Holy'.

Such adoration is expressed through their "casting down their golden crowns around the glassy sea". The temptation and ability to crown oneself as literally 'king' of the castle of existence, is rejected, and instead the bowing down of worship becomes the position to seek – placing oneself into the ocean of the life of the Trinity.

"Cherubim and Seraphim falling down before thee" – the celestial hierarchy, all those ordered ranks, find a common life in worship which brings every vocation into the life of God, through the joining of the ecclesiastical hierarchy in the common refrain: 'Holy, Holy, Holy'.

In the Book of Revelation we are told that they all bow down before the Throne to be raised up with new life. In such adoration past, present and future are joined in one who "was and is, and evermore shall be". Worship is to consciously place ourselves within eternity, and thus be given confidence to resist the temptation to over magnify the present and undervalue past and future. Each of the perspectives needs to be acknowledged in order for worship to enter into the freedom of the majesty of the Trinity.

But the journey is not simple or straightforward. Despite a commitment to the continuing refrain 'Holy, Holy, Holy', there needs to be recognition of the reality that there is 'darkness' which can be seen to hide or obscure God and the invitation to live in His Trinitarian goodness. We are full of weeds and blight, due to our own limitations, and as the result of forces we can neither understand nor control. To feel disconnected is part of the journey, even as we sing the refrain of the Trinity. In the mystery of Jesus we can notice that as well as His encounters which bring light and hope, He continually moves on "to the next village". That is, He is absent as well as present. Those who encounter Him have to live with His apparent absence, and need to find ways in which His love can be remembered as a continuing source of comfort. This reality of absence and apparent darkness points to the particular importance of a liturgical framework to ensure that whatever the mood or experience, disciples needs a commitment to put themselves into the song of the church which celebrates the presence and power of the Trinity.

Our darkness is a reflection of human failing and fallibility, which might seem to 'hide' God's presence, but in fact He is always seeking to offer warmth and light. Our challenge is to trust that gifting when seemingly overwhelmed by needing to own the place of brokenness to renew our schemes and systems. Hence the powerful poetic insight. "Though the eye of sinful man Thy glory may not see".

Yet the reality remains "only Thou art holy, there is none beside Thee". There is only one source of life giving warmth and light – which we are called to trust. "There is none beside Thee" echoes the clear message of Jesus whenhe proclaims that "I am the way, the truth and the life". Worship is to focus upon this one way, this one presence and this one invitation since this way, is "perfect in power, in love and purity". Once again the relationship of persons modelled in the Trinity, into which we are invited, highlights the fact that love and power need to be perfectly aligned, for individuals as much as for society to flourish. From such alignment comes the purity of those hearts who shall see God (Matthew 5).

And thus the crescendo returns, to ensure that worship which has embraced the creedal heights and depths of God's call and human desires will remain focussed upon 'Holy, Holy, Holy' to enable encounter with 'The Lord God Almighty' in a manner that knows the deep purpose of this complex flow of creation: so that "all Thy works shall praise Thy name, in earth and sky and sea".

This is the doctrine and expression of living in the Trinity. All is made for praise as the means of participation. Even parts that might be judged to be unseemly and disconnected according to the limited perspective of a particular human experience.

Again the emphasis upon being 'merciful and mighty': love and power is the key – and therefore the real agenda for every act of worship. Each creature receives power in the form of life. How we organise, accumulate or share power is determinative of the identities we pursue and the societies we design. Too often love is relegated towards personal and group relations – the more love is scaled down, the easier it can seem to identify and handle.

Yet persons are those creatures made for love to sound through them, in every kind of relationship. It is love which is power in the way of the Trinity. Sadly the human instinct for survival is wary of trying to live in such an open way, where the needs of others dictate the agenda – such as the victim in the 'way' of the Good Samaritan. Rather, as most famously highlighted by Thomas Hobbes, the instinct for survival becomes power that needs to be managed by law. Hence the human rights movement in our own times.

Only by living in the Trinity can love be infused with a confidence that enables us to become the primary currency connecting human beings. Relationships of love create the graceful energy we can identify in particular responses to disaster appeals – hope and faith suddenly made manifest. The missionary task is to form such 'moments' into something more normative. Still realistic about the continuing darkness which seems to hide love and encourage power to be exercised for more limited and precise means: but becoming so steeped in the song of "Holy, Holy, Holy" that this is the sound of love made power which rings through all those who join in the refrain of worship.

Heber had a very short ministry in India. Yet he laid the foundations for a Christian presence, a tradition of learning and a gracious friendship with those of other faiths following different systems. The light has continued to shine amidst considerable experience of gloom and setback. Here is a model for discipleship, so beautifully expressed in the evocative poetry of his great hymn that provides a foundation and a framework for Christian discipleship. Worship that ever seeks to give praise: Holy, Holy, Holy – one perfect in mercy and might – Blessed Trinity. Here all of life can be embraced in perfect wholeness. Labour pains will always be part of the journey – but descent from our own comforts is so often the path of being broken open to know more purity. The importance of poetry in a world obsessed with the precision of prose: a way of creating the perfect harmony which is salvation for creation.

Holy. Holy. Holy: merciful and mighty.

God in three persons, blessed Trinity.